HALF-OPEN WINDOWS

HALF-OPEN WINDOWS

GANESH MATKARI

Translated from the Marathi
by **Jerry Pinto**

SPEAKING
TIGER

SPEAKING TIGER PUBLISHING PVT. LTD
4381/4, Ansari Road, Daryaganj
New Delhi 110002

Originally published in Marathi by Samakalin Prakashan in 2014
Published in English by Speaking Tiger in paperback 2017

ISBN: 978-93-86338-35-8
eISBN: 978-93-86338-36-5

10 9 8 7 6 5 4 3 2 1

Typeset in Cardo Regular by SÜRYA, New Delhi
Printed at Thomson Press India Ltd.

Author's dedication

For Pallavi, for all the possible reasons.

'All this happened, more or less.'

—Kurt Vonnegut, *Slaughterhouse Five*

CONTENTS

BREAK

It was nine thirty in the morning by the time I got to the funnies in the *Mirror*. Sanika's SMS—'Rchd office'—had just made my phone vibrate. Sanika adores short messaging. I do not find it necessary to announce, 'Reached Such-and-Such' or 'Doing so-and-so' or 'Leaving in 10' or to even be informed of that kind of thing. In a city like Mumbai, you have to factor in some unpredictability. It is now a fact of life that traffic or trains will delay you or a rickshawalla won't take you where you want to go. So what's the use of keeping track of who's going to be late and by how many minutes? And we don't live close to the station. In Evershine Nagar, half the problem is the last mile. On top of that, the rains are here. Getting to work on time means a battle with unwilling rickshaw- or taxi-drivers and then the Chinese torture of a dripping train carriage.

But there's no use telling Sanika any of this. She lets me know her entire timetable, amendments included. Even now, a long message is waiting as it always is: 'Got such-and-so train, rchd @ dis time, afternoon meeting wid da consultant postponed, mayb l8', etc.

And as always, I reply with an okay and a smiley stuck on.

Actually, Sanika has no need to use the trains. I cannot understand why a partner in an architectural firm the size of SNA should find it a bore to drive her own car. But that phrase—'a bore'—is mine.

According to Sanika, she has too much on her mind to concentrate properly on driving. If you ask me, you don't need concentration to drive. It's a reflex. One drives on auto-pilot, as if by a routine so fixed that should it need changing, the situation is already so bad that one's skill has not much chance of saving one's life. If this were not the case, if driving truly takes skill and concentration, how do countless people steer their cars through traffic even as they listen to third-class Hindi film songs and the meaningless babble of RJs? Or chat on their cell phones? So Sanika's refusal to drive herself probably arises out of her not wanting to. And so the car is largely mine to use even if it is in her name.

Mirror done, I turn to *Times Ascent*. 9:30 a.m. I have time. It was only three months ago that I quit my job as a lecturer in an engineering college. I had no idea what I wanted to do but I was bored. I found it difficult to teach students who had no real interest in learning. I didn't want to sit around and moan about my lack of job satisfaction.

Sanika too felt it was better for me to quit than for her to bear my complaints about my work. I had hoped that the excellent marks with which I had finished my

BE (Civil) would mean that I would be snapped up by some hot architectural firm or real-estate developer but there was no sign of that happening. However, I had finished my education a while ago and my work experience was only academic. Besides, the job market is in bad shape. The Japanese and Chinese companies are now so fashionable in engineering and architecture that Indian companies are struggling to survive. Thankfully, SNA is one of the exceptions. It's doing well and that means we're doing well too.

I have a standing offer from Sanika to join the SNA project management team.

She had got together with two of her college friends and started SNA; it was now one of the up-and-coming architectural firms. They were in demand and the realty magazines had run several features on them. But from my limited social interactions with her partners, I knew that they were likely to be arrogant. I didn't think I could work with them. And Sanika was one of the bosses. One of my fears was that our relationship might not survive my working under her. Even if we had fallen in love with each other in college and had lived together for four years afterwards, a live-in relationship is a live-in relationship is a live-in relationship. How long would it take to end, should that thought occur to either of us? Playing at being modern, we hadn't married but the insecurity of our relationship was a Sword of Damocles hanging over our heads. Or maybe it didn't hang over Sanika's head. That has nothing to do with the self-confidence SNA's success brought with it; it's just who she is.

~

The intercom's loud buzz startled me. Robie began to bark too as I got up. I hoped no one had called to complain to the society's offices.

'Sahib, courier.'

'Send him up,' I said. Affluent housing societies such as ours place a high premium on security but nothing is foolproof. Every day, the newspapers tell us how little such security services can secure, other than the desks at which they sit. But then perhaps it has something to do with this slogan I read somewhere along the highway: 'The best break is a mental break'. Perhaps the security industry believes that the best security is the feeling of security and so the uniformed guards, intercoms, hefty monthly outgoings, all represent today's version of mental security. By that standard, you might say we were very safe indeed.

By the time I had hushed Robie, the bell rang. A clerical-looking young man in a blue raincoat was at the door. The water from his raincoat had formed a miniature lake around him. One look at Robie's attack stance and he took two steps back.

'He's tied up,' I said.

The courier laughed weakly but stayed put. I wasn't surprised. Robie is a German Shepherd. He may be young, but he looks powerful and loves to bark. The courier extended his hand and gave me two or three envelopes and a sheet to sign. 'Signature and telephone number, please,' he said.

Nothing important; just the usual mailers from banks. However, it occurred to me that everyone from Sanika to the courier was at work and here I was, still unwashed. I set the papers aside and the bell rang again. Perhaps the courier had forgotten his pen, I thought, and opened the door to be confronted by Joshi Kaku.

Our society prides itself on being thoroughly cosmopolitan. Other than Joshi Kaku who lives on the seventeenth floor, I do not know any other Maharashtrians who live in our society. Of course this does not prove that no other Marathi people live here. I'm not the kind of person to go looking for them. Besides, there are more than five hundred other flats in the society and discovering which ones belong to Marathis seems impossible; they all would be busy with their own lives. Anyway, in the two years that I have lived here, she is the only Marathi person I have encountered.

'Yesterday Robie scratched Banjo again,' Kaku said. 'You really shouldn't let him off his leash.'

Kaku's jeremiad had begun. Most of our interactions with Joshi Kaku are about Robie and Banjo. Banjo is the Joshi pet, a fat cat with fur the colour of stippled ash. He's fourteen or fifteen years old. In feline years, he's ancient. He can only see out of one eye and limps. By and large, cats are just a little too clever for their own good. Banjo can never see Robie without hissing. At that venerable age, should one be let out of the house? (I don't mean Joshi Kaku.) But no, all day long Banjo is allowed to roam freely; he returns to the Joshi flat only to eat. Contrariwise, Robie is locked up in the house all day.

I take him for a walk every evening in the podium garden and let him off the leash for a while. He's good with children and loves to play. Which is why he tries to play with Banjo. Their first encounter ended with bloodshed on both sides.

That day Joshi Kaku presented herself at our door with a bandaged Banjo in her arms and proceeded to heap coals of fire upon our heads. This set the tone for our relationship. Every few days Robie would try to befriend Banjo, they would fight and that night or the next morning, Kaku and Banjo would be at our door. The first couple of times, Sanika was deeply affected. She suggested a number of radical solutions, from returning Robie to finding another home. Then she got used to it too. From the beginning I had decided that I was not going to pay much attention to Joshi Kaku so I wasted no emotion on her. Her warnings continued unabated. Some time ago, her one and only son had come down on a visit from Chicago. He was deputed to talk to us. He was a nice guy and somewhat apologetic. He told us that he had been trying to get Joshi Kaku to go to the US but she would not go without her cat and taking Banjo to America meant paperwork that he was unwilling to get into. *And* his wife was allergic to cats. I wasn't sure I believed in this allergy. In my opinion, it was a feeble attempt at assuaging the guilt he felt about abandoning his mother, but I nodded my head in supportive mode. As he left, he scratched Robie behind his ear and said, 'Good doggie' and then asked me not to take his mother's complaints too seriously.

Seriously, me?

But here she was again.

'Your Robie is going to kill Banjo one day,' she was saying when I tuned back in. As always, I tried to pacify her. But now I was getting late. I had agreed to meet Ranga Giridhari at the Energee stand in front of Express Towers at 1:30. Ranga Giridhari is a college buddy, from the architecture branch. He was Sanika's classmate. His real name is Rangnath Giridhar Gokhale. To blend in with cosmopolitan Mumbai, he cut his name in half. When he finished a post-graduate degree at the London School of Design, he took a pledge to speak with a British-Marathi accent. The name 'Ranga' might suggest a maverick but he always wore formals with rimless glasses that cost about twenty-five thousand rupees. He was a VP-Design at DLF and had agreed to put in a word for me in Projects or Business Development. He only had some 'finer points' about the job he wanted to clarify with me. This was what we were supposed to discuss today but until Kaku returned to the seventeenth floor, I would not be able to leave and I hadn't had a bath yet.

'He's been with me since he was born. Fourteen years, see? He's like a child to me,' Kaku said, ignoring the human child in the US who must have hiccupped at being so summarily overlooked.

'Kaku, Robie does not do this intentionally. He only wants to play,' I said, following the routine.

But she wasn't in the mood to listen.

'He's just waiting for Banjo to die; then he can have his own sweet way,' she snapped.

That way, we're all used to Kaku's melodrama. But who'll say no to a little free entertainment? Even now, the homemaker next door will be giving her sister-in-law on the third floor all the gory details. Just then, the door across from us opened and Bunty popped his head out. As always he had a towel tied securely around his waist. Don't go by his name. Bunty is a full-grown lad in his thirties. I'm not sure that he ever wears clothes when he's at home. And he is always at home and always swathed in a towel. But then he lives alone. He must be from an affluent family to be able to afford a flat in our building. Someone told me a while ago that Bunty works as a pilot in Kingfisher Airlines. That explains his odd hours. Who knows what the truth of the matter is. With Kingfisher in the condition it is, no wonder he's in the condition he is. Always at home, I mean. Anyway, who am I to cast the first stone? I've been home alone ever since I gave up my job. Perhaps he wonders about me too. But I have one thing over him—I wear clothes at home. I tried to control my smile but Joshi Kaku caught it and this set off a fresh explosion.

'You watch it. I'll go to the police. My nephew is in the CBI, mind it!'

Whenever she trots out her CBI connections, I wonder

whether they have no better work than to defend ageing tomcats.

Somehow I managed to get rid of her, closed the door and scuttled off for a bath. On the way, I stopped to check the status of my Torrent downloads. All four stuck on 35 per cent. I shouldn't have set all four to download simultaneously, of course. Am I going to watch all four at the same time? But hey, it's about having them on your hard drive, right? I added a Stephen King audio book to the configuration and went to the bathroom.

~

It was 1:45 when I began my hunt for a parking space outside the NCPA. It was drizzling so I didn't want to park too far away. I knew that I shouldn't have brought the car because parking is a nightmare in these parts. But driving is a bad habit I can't shake.

When I was leaving, my phone showed that there had already been three or four missed calls from Ranga. I sent him an SMS to say I'd be late to avoid answering. When I couldn't find a parking space, I handed the car over to the valet at the Oberoi Trident and went into the lobby and called Ranga. He replied with four invaluable words: 'Meeting. Call you back.'

I sent him a text: 'Come to the Trident lobby,' and called Sanika.

While Sanika likes to send out streams of SMSes, it's even odds that she'll answer her phone. She's always in a meeting, at a briefing, or in a design workshop. What time is left over, she spends with her partners or her juniors. And when she's with them, she never picks up her phone.

Why not? No reason. It's just of those things with her. Picking up the phone is for those filler times. When she's between conferences, or someone is late, you get the picture. So it was a surprise when she picked up on the first ring.

'Hi Sushrut,' she said in her everyday voice. 'Where are you? Met Ranga?'

'No yaar. I got late. Kaku came with Banjo and stuck like a leech.'

'*Arre baa-aa-ap re!*' said Sanika, her voice grave. This means nothing. Whatever happens, Sanika's default response is '*Arre baap re!*'—an all-purpose exclamation that generally suggests surprise and sympathy for some minor upset. From a delayed train to a sudden death, she finds this one response suffices. The result is that someone who does not know her well might assume on hearing her saying this that her father had just died. At SNA, they still tell the story of how when she heard the news over the phone that her father had indeed just died she said, '*Arre baap re*' in just that way and Antya ignored it and continued to shove a slice of his son's birthday cake at her. By the way, Antya is Anant Redij, the A in SNA.

'Nothing so dramatic. He's not dead. Not yet anyway,' I said, lightening the tone deliberately, for the discussion seemed to have become serious.

'Okay, tell me one thing,' Sanika said, her tone now

verging on the secretive, 'What if you were to not work for a while?'

'And do what? Cook?'

'Don't be silly. You've been saying for a while that you want to try your hand at creative writing, right? Anyway you have time on your hands now and things are going well here. So why rush about looking for a job? I was going to tell you yesterday. We're expecting a big account to come through. Then I thought, better mention it only when it's confirmed.'

'It's a thought,' I said. 'Let's talk in the evening.'

'Another thing,' Sanika said. That got my attention. I live in dread of Sanika's 'another thing'-s. Her '*baap re*'-s may have been diluted through constant use but her 'another thing'-s presage something radical.

'Since we're talking about the new account, I thought I'd mention it,' she said. 'We've been appointed to build three seven-star hotels in the US. For the Rednecks Group. The designs, the specs, the BOQ, everything's final. We were waiting for the clients' sign-off. We just got the confirmation.'

'Congrats,' I said cautiously. By the way, BOQ is realty-speak for Bills of Quantities.

'One problem. For the first six months, they want someone there to get it going, to coordinate with their Seattle head office. Until things settle down, you know. Originally Antya was going. But he has a family emergency on his hands. So I'll have to go next month.'

'Can't Agashe go?'

It was a weak attempt. Agashe is Niranjan Agashe, N in SNA.

'Agashe?' she asked as if I were missing a few screws. 'He handles all the biggies here. Who's going to get the permissions and suchlike through the Corporation? Partho is there, true, but he hasn't got Agashe's experience. No, displacing Agashe is just not on.'

I was silent. I knew she was right.

'Hello, Sushrut? Are you still there?' Sanika asked.

'I'm here,' I said. What I didn't say was that a huge hollow had developed where my stomach had been. Sanika off for six months? What did she really want to say? Was she saying, 'I have to go' or was she saying 'Let's go'? Why would she say the latter? Why would SNA pay for two people? So she's going alone? For six months? Would our relationship survive? On what? What if she met someone there? What if the contract were extended? Anyway, there was nothing holding us together. I began to remember all the things I had repressed: Aai telling us to get married and how Sanika and I would laugh away her suggestions; those couples who wandered arm in arm in college and then married someone else for the sheer convenience of it; my sister's love marriage, an unsteady and unreliable thing. These began to drift in a slide show before my eyes…and suddenly I realized why Sanika had brought up my creative writing aspirations. She was not going alone. Au contraire, I was to go to the US with her and play housewife, sorry, homemaker, sit-at-home spouse awaiting the breadwinner's return, holding the fort, doing the odd jobs and squeezing in a little writing. But looked at another way, how different would that be from my life now? I wasn't trying to write, true, but for the rest? Was my sense of security an illusion? Sanika kept talking but I couldn't hear what she was saying. She seemed to be excited, almost elated, and that made me a little angry. Not that I understood why. What was wrong with this? I was going with my capable wife, no, my capable partner, to America for six months, during which time I could try and turn my hobby into a career. What could be wrong with that? What's to resent? I had never been much of a believer in the male ego. If that had been my operating principle, how could I have lived with Sanika this long?

'Ranga's here. I'll call you later,' I said and ended the call abruptly. No lie there. Ranga had arrived. But I knew, even before I raised my finger from the button, I shouldn't have hung up. How much of this was love for Sanika and how much of it was burgeoning insecurity, I could not have said then. Should I have offered strong opposition right there? Should I have threatened to end whatever we had at that point? But how? I had no job, no home of my own, no one else to call my own in this city. My parents, sure. But they were in Pune. I could go there, I suppose.

Seeing Ranga made me feel a little better. He was a good friend but in that moment it wasn't just his friendship that warmed me but also the reassurance he represented. When something happens over which you have no control, it is good to see that some things don't change. Ranga's spiffy clothes were a sign that the world was still the same and so I hurried up, wanting to chat with him as of old. But Sanika had raised some weird questions in my head. Coming clean was the only way forward so I told him all.

'Congratulations,' he said and after he shook my hand, he immediately sent Sanika an SMS. And she, of course, replied just as quickly.

'Why congratulate me?' I mumbled. 'What did I have to do with it?'

'Don't be silly. I'm congratulating you on your excellent choice in wives,' he said and thumped me on the back. This is one of Ranga's most irritating habits: he must hit you. Calling Sanika my wife is another. And since he was her classmate, he has been calling her that since our third year in college. He says legal status be damned, you have to look at the emotions in a relationship.

In other words, we didn't discuss too many 'finer points' that day. Neither of us felt like it. Since he seemed in a good mood, my problems, whose reality I had anyway begun to doubt after talking to Ranga, faded and we went to Frangipani and he ordered beer. I don't drink when I'm driving, not because my driving is affected but because of the random police checks. Since they're rarely on the prowl at 4 p.m., my refusals might not have been as wholehearted as usual. Giving half an ear to his non-stop monologue, I began to stare past the plate glass windows at the chafa tree, dripping rain. After two beers, Ranga made a celebratory phone call to Sanika and plucking her from a meeting, talked to her for twenty minutes. From his side of the conversation, I figured out that I had been right. She was expecting me to go with her but was waiting for the client confirmation. She was confident it would come. I took the phone from Ranga and talked to her for two minutes too but she was cautious. She wasn't sure what I was feeling but she knew that something was up with me. We agreed that we would talk when she got home that night. Late that night, for she was going to go straight from her meeting to a client's drinks-and-dinner thing for his daughter's engagement. Antya would drop her home, she said. She did suggest, as a formality, that I come too. The invitation said, 'with family'. But she knew that it wasn't my thing so she didn't push.

~

On my way home, I kept thinking about this. So much so that I found it impossible to concentrate on the audio book I had downloaded the day before.

On top of that, I had the frightening thought that if I were really serious about creative writing, I should stop listening to these trashy bestsellers and start downloading Palahniuk, Rushdie and other literary types instead. So I took out my earphones and concentrated on driving but that didn't work too long. Odd thoughts began to surface. I had always said that I could drive by reflex but now it was clear that reflexes don't work if your head is not on straight. But that applies to pretty much everything else in life, not just driving. You can manage on reflexes as long as things are going your way. But when something unexpected happens and things seem in danger of slipping out of control, that's when you end up a mess. This must have been the beers talking. Almost without thinking, I stepped on the brakes. I got the car to the side of the road and stuck my earphones in again.

By the time I'd got past the snarls and tangles of the traffic en route to the western suburbs, it was 6:30. As the lift doors opened, I heard Robie's bark. Walk-time. I checked the Torrent download status and added the audio book of Murakami's *A Wild Sheep Chase*, drank a glass of water and went downstairs.

As usual the garden was busy. I walked two rounds of the society and then slipped Robie off his leash so he could play with the children. He raced off into the wet grass. I looked around for somewhere to sit. There was Joshi Kaku on the bench at the edge of the garden… probably trying to ensure Banjo's safety from Robie. I went and sat down next to her. She did not look at me. It seemed she had still not calmed down.

'I don't see Banjo about?' I made an attempt at conversation.

'He's gone,' she said, still looking away into the distance.

For a couple of seconds, this did not register. Gone? Where? When? And then I understood.

'Gone?' Although I'd got what she meant, I pretended ignorance.

'Yes,' she turned to me for the first time and said, 'It was time. He'd been ill for several days. I should have kept him at home, looked after him better. I did try but shutting him up seemed to make it worse. So I let him out, what to do? Don't worry. I'm not blaming you or Robie. I expected this. When he was so still this afternoon, I took him to the vet...'

Her voice broke. Perhaps she had even now, just returned from the vet. I was blank. What does one say at times like these?

'Told Makarand?' I said for want of anything else to say. By some stroke of good fortune, her son's name came back at the nick of time.

'No. I'll email him tonight. He's been after me for so long to come to America. I've been saying no, using Banjo as an excuse. What will I do there? I'll have nothing to do.'

Now I could see tears in her eyes. I never thought I would hear this tone in her voice and so I just shut up. And then the phone began to vibrate in my hands. Sanika and Antya had arrived at the cocktails do. She promised 'wl try 2 get bk soon'. Then 'we cd discuss our plans'. I did not reply and just sat there. In front of me, Robie romped with the children. Joshi Kaku sat looking quietly into the distance.

And darkness fell.

TIME

No matter where you are, you are as comfortable as you want to be; at least, that's my experience. It may not be everyone else's. Some people find themselves out of sorts as soon as they leave the zone of the familiar. Look at Sushrut. There are certain kinds of places where he's comfortable. But outside his libraries and coffee shops and electronics stores, he's virtually lost. Taking him anywhere means you have to use a combination of kicking and coaxing. Specially places where he might have to…oh horrors…encounter people. And what if he had to get to know them?

Just the atmosphere of over-priced places like five- or seven-star hotels is enough to give him a complex. But if I try to say something, he's all, 'Sanika, you know what I'm like, right?' And he's home safe. As if being the way he is, is a justification in itself. It's not as if he's some 'high-thinking-and-simple-living' type either. From computers to bread, it's brands, brands, brands, all the way for this guy. His personal paradox, I suppose. It might be the shades of his bourgeois upbringing too but I'm not so sure.

I won't say that my background is elite or progressive either. My father was a captain in the army. I was born in Mumbai but I never really lived here; didn't study here either. So living in new and different places, fitting in comfortably and confidently, is something of a habit for me. This has been of some benefit. In a field like architecture, which is getting more difficult and demanding by the day, handling clients has become even more important than design.

It isn't just chance that my partners at SNA, Antya and Agashe, have begun to leave most of the PR decisions to me. While everyone knows that this is an important aspect of our work, it often goes unacknowledged. And I end up not doing the kind of work I'd like to but spending my time at meetings, conferences and dinners. So I work and work but often end the day feeling that my time has been wasted.

Take today. The majority of it went in conference calls and now here we are at Lalvani's daughter's engagement. One more PR thing and another day done and dusted. And so it goes.

This is one day I would have liked to get home early. The Rednecks Group deal, a big juicy one, was finalized today. I am to spend the next six months in Seattle at their group headquarters. That's the breaking news. The best part is Sushrut comes with me. I wanted to celebrate with him today. But when I told him, he freaked out. Who knows what goes on in his head?

I'd have liked to go home straight and find out but

duty calls so here we are. When Antya went to the loo, I dashed off a text to Sushrut to say I'd got to the hotel. Then I wandered around the lobby for a bit. I like the JW lobby. A lot. It's not just the height. Nowadays every five-star has an atrium-style lobby. But JW has managed, somehow (how?), to make this huge space warm and cosy. Maybe it's the abundance of wood panelling, the huge paintings behind the reception, the use of fabrics… something. I can't put my finger on it but the overall impact is wonderful. I made a note to find out the name of their interior design consultant and Antya arrived.

'Come on, let's get this over with,' he said, adjusting his cufflinks. I followed him.

Antya has looked tired all day but that's no surprise. Ever since the complaints have begun coming from Rohan's school, he's been worried. He spent the most of the day closeted with the principal. Yes, there's a wife. Aarti. But frankly, she just can't handle any of this.

I am a bit surprised by the whole thing. Rohan seems like a bright kid to me. Not as academically inclined and sorted as Antya, perhaps. But where does an academic inclination help anyone get on in life? Street smarts are more than enough. And when does everything work out the way you want it?

There's a time for everything, and a moment when it will come. But will Antya listen? And when it's about your kid? That's a whole new ball game. The parents or guardians I know, however well-meaning, never try to put themselves into the shoes of the young. They never try to remember what it was like at that age. When I consider Antya's state, I'm rather pleased that I did not get stuck with the regular one-marriage-two-kids package. I have no pressures, no responsibilities. Who knows if I would have been given this kind of freedom if I had been with someone other than Sushrut? He may have his quirks but he more than makes up for those.

'Did you see Swarupa?' Antya asked, and for a moment, I was startled.

'Swarupa? Here?'

'In the Marriott? You must be joking. She was giving a speech at the morcha outside the gate. About Lalvani. Where our LL Residency banners were hanging? She was standing right there. You really didn't see her?'

A fine line appeared on Antya's brow.

'No. Means, I saw the morcha, not her,' I said as casually as I could.

'Surprising,' he said with a laugh. 'Your nemesis and you didn't see her?'

'No need for melodrama,' I said. 'What do you mean: Nemesis?' I said it but I knew it was weak. Actually, Swarupa and I do have some history. But I don't think I did anything wrong. Even now when I think back I don't think I should have behaved any differently. But who knows...?

~

I met Swarupa Karkhanis ten years ago. A few years before that, I had been working as a junior architect in the small practice that Dorab Mistry, one of our visiting faculty members in college, still maintained. The practice was truly small because Mistry was semi-retired. His real interest lay in teaching. But some old clients, his friends really, found work for him to do. Generally interiors but there were a few Parsi clients who wanted bungalows built near Gholvad. He was also building his own bungalow there. The work proceeded at a leisurely pace. We kept ourselves busy all day and then at the stroke of 5 p.m., we left. Literally at the stroke of five because Mistry had brought his great-grandfather's grandfather clock to the office since he had no place for it at home. It was in this office that I had met Swarupa for the first time. She had started coming there with Premendra.

~

As Antya and I made our way past the banquets, I pushed all these thoughts to the back of my mind in order to focus on the work at hand. Ask my mother what work I do and she'll tell you that I leave poor Sushrut at home and swan about at parties. But it is the performances at these parties rather than the work we do in the office that bring in the next jobs—at least in my experience. It isn't only your host you come to meet; it's the entire building industry that turns up here: builders, CEOs, their buddies, their wives and children, the architects in corporate design teams, chief engineers…all present and correct. And in this field, there are four or five major companies among which you can jump. If you leave a job with one of them, you join another with a ridiculously large package. From there on to the third or maybe back to the first.

This means that everyone knows everyone else. And it also means that even in the few seconds between recognizing people and greeting them, you've got to run over their past and present. Not just the names but who they're with, their position in the hierarchy and if high enough, the names of spouse and children...and so on and so forth. To keep all these records straight and to summon them up at a moment's notice is not easy. Antya and I have trained ourselves to do it. But today Antya is a bit out of it. So I have to be on full alert.

Even as this occurs to me, my phone vibrates. Can't be Sushrut. He doesn't text unless he has a reason. And now, I reckon, he's in the garden with Robie, our dog. Or he's downloading some more films from the internet. Who knows when he's ever going to watch them all?

I took my phone out of my purse and found I was right. Not Sushrut. An unknown number.

'Want 2 meet u. Where r u? SK'

SK is Swarupa Karkhanis.

For a couple of minutes, I was stumped. Antya was talking to Bombay Dyeing's new design veep. The Lalvani Group's elder daughter-in-law, who doubles as the Biz Dev head, Priya Lalvani, was making her way over, waving a greeting.

'So nice of you to come, darling,' she cooed at me. I gave her back darling for darling while figuring out how to get clear. Luckily, it wasn't too difficult. It was peak time for guests to arrive and as host, Priya had to meet and greet them all. It was her duty to keep the peace and get everyone to ignore the protesters at the gate who were voicing their opposition to the LL Residency Project that we had designed and which was to come up on what had been slum land. As usual, we made small talk about the rain, the traffic and the pollution. She commended the strong aesthetic sense we had showed in Elena, our under-construction project that had just showed up on Colaba's skyline. Just when we began to run out of topics, a big fish swam into her ken and she rushed off with a quick 'Enjoy' in my direction.

I was free.

It took another ten minutes to free Antya and steer him to a place we could talk.

'Are you feeling all right? Is everything okay? What's happened to you?' he asked as we edged our way out, flicking smiles, left and right. Somehow we made it out and parked ourselves at a small round table outside the coffee shop. I presented the phone to a confused Antya.

'SK? Who's that?' Antya asked. He would. He hadn't worked with Swarupa earlier so he didn't know her SMS style. But he was no fool. In the next second, he'd guessed. Perhaps my worried expression clued him in.

'SK? Swarupa. Swarupa, right? What does she want?'

'How would I know?' I asked, irritated.

'No, how would you? But this can't be good, right?'

'No.'

I was trying to guess why she wanted to meet me but it wasn't easy.

~

Premendra was one of Dorab Mistry's ex-students and as such, he began to visit the office. But soon he was friends with everyone, from the three or four junior architects to the senior architect Rahul Mehta. The other senior, Diwakar Panchal, had been his classmate.

Premendra was my senior by about seven or eight years. He had graduated from our college but was not practising. He had taken slum redevelopment schemes as his thesis topic but he had gotten so involved that he'd got a whole lot of scholarships and fellowships and had spent the next few years going to various countries to study low-cost housing projects. Some years in, he had founded an NGO called SEHAT (*S*olutions for *E*conomic *H*ealth *A*nd *T*olerance). This name fascinated us. As his classmate, Panchal reserved the right to tease Premendra. He renamed SEHAT as Slum Housing for Indian Tenants or SHIT.

It was an in-joke for a small group, for Premendra was slowly growing in stature. He had begun to be called to various high-profile seminars as a speaker. His photograph had begun to appear in newspapers alongside those of politicians. To us, he was just Panchal's classmate and Mistry's ex-student. But he was also eager to sign on as a client.

He had just decided to take on the responsibility for

completing his pet project in Vikhroli and our office was to be the coordinating agency. Looking at the size of Lokmanya Nagar, several builders had begun to slaver at the jaws. But SEHAT chose Pant-Prabhu as developers and Dorab Mistry & Associates as architects. Mistry was the first to say that this was not a good idea. The practice was small and no one had any desire to grow it. But Premendra was resolute. He did not want a company that might force him to compromise on his vision or ideals. He wanted to build a prototype that would privilege community interaction over profit and that would put SEHAT's name on the low-cost housing map. His enthusiasm was infectious; Rahul and Panchal took charge and we were off.

Our contact at SEHAT was Swarupa.

~

'So what have you decided?' Antya asked.

To meet or not to meet? I had not made up my mind. I got up and stood by the curtain glazing. From there, I could see the crowd at the door. She must be there, somewhere among them.

Swarupa and I became fast friends quickly and remained friends for quite a while. There was nothing surprising about this. I have people skills, even if I say so myself, and she was also quite nice. She was originally Swarupa Saraf. Her education was also quite remarkable. She had done a diploma in civil engineering and then a BA and an MA in sociology. Her family members were of the opinion that she was destined to be an eternal student, unwilling to try and prove herself in the real world. But she defied their gloomy predictions too. She began to work with many different NGOs. She quickly gained a reputation as someone who could deliver even under difficult circumstances and as a woman of quick decisions. She also found time to marry a struggling actor, Aniruddh Karkhanis, one year younger than she. She met Premendra at a Land Development Conference at Jaipur and a little while later, she joined SEHAT. As the projects increased, the need was felt for another architect as Swarupa found it difficult to handle everything. And this was when she approached me, suggesting it might be a smart career move. I saw her point and almost overnight I was at SEHAT. Things began to go downhill after that.

~

The crowds outside the hotel began to increase. The banner-bearers were still manning their positions but their numbers were now being swelled by the idlers of the area.

The OB vans were there now, their antennae poking above the heads of the crowd. I pressed my nose against the glass to get a better view, it was too far away and already dark. The floodlights had not been turned on. Deliberately? To keep the crowds down? Who knew?

'What do you want to do?' Antya asked. 'Should we leave?'

'No. I think I should talk to her. You go back.'

'Sure? I know something went down between you two. She bad-mouths you quite openly. That government-funded hospital project? Remember what happened to it? We lost a big job because of that stupid woman.'

'And because of me,' I said. 'I think we'd have got it if I hadn't been representing SNA.'

'I didn't mean it that way.'

'I know. Go back to the party. Meet the usual suspects. I'll take five.'

'Okay,' he said and hared off, as if liberated. He doesn't like any kind of unpredictability. Not that I love it but I can handle it better.

I went to the glass and looked out again. The floods were on and by their light I could see a black bubbling of umbrellas. It must have begun to rain. I could see my face reflected in the glass, backlit.

I sat down at the table, ordered a cappuccino and began to play with my mobile. It wasn't difficult to guess why Swarupa wanted to meet me. She wanted info perhaps… About the LL Residency? What we'd done to get the project passed? The dodges we'd tried, the shortcuts we'd used? I knew that she was ready to use any means to get her work done. But I found it equally difficult to believe that she would be willing to use our history to her own ends.

I knew that arm-twisting was one of her weapons but I couldn't imagine the Swarupa I knew adding emotional blackmail to her arsenal.

~

My first six months in SEHAT went well. Swarupa and I made good progress. The basic approvals were all in hand and work had started at the site. Premendra was happy. During this period, Swarupa was happy too. Aniruddh had landed a role in a much-talked-about saas-bahu-type serial, not the lead role but one that offered some scope for his talent. The money was good and people had begun to recognize him on the street. It seemed as if they were settling down. Then Swarupa got pregnant and was in seventh heaven. I have some good memories of this time, memories that have survived the debacle that followed. Hours spent outside the BMC office chatting about this and that; the various ploys we devised to get the authorities' sign-off since Premendra had a 'no-bribes' policy; eating ragda puri at the famous bhelwala at Khodadad Circle after we'd been late at the office; that kind of thing.

But that summer I fell ill and everything changed. At first this was good for a joke or two, but the bouts of illness began to get worse and I began a round of doctors and tests.

I realized this first when I resumed after a week's sick leave. The doctors couldn't say exactly what was wrong with me but I kept losing weight. Sushrut and I had been in love since college, the only discussion was to marry or not to marry, something we didn't discuss with each other but with both sets of parents. We felt: if you love someone, you don't need to marry to live together. They felt: people have to get married anyway so why didn't we? And even though we were not living together yet, we were frequently at each other's homes. It was he who first dragged me to a doctor. And he kept a stern eye on me to make sure I followed doctor's orders. When Sushrut heard that the doctors had suggested that my condition might be aggravated by the heat and dust of site visits, he told Premendra and got me exempted. Again on doctor's orders, I was forced to take leave. Swarupa knew I was unwell. I was sure she would keep up the pace of the work at the site. Maybe I was too wrapped up in my own illness. Maybe I should have called her up to understand what was going on in her life. Maybe I had been so certain that things were going well with her that I hadn't asked. It was on the day that I returned from leave that I first found out about her troubles. But by then, it was already too late.

That day I arrived at office and was stopped short at the door. Premendra's cabin was in front of the reception. Personally, I don't like the idea of the boss's cabin right up front; but often it can be a useful position to occupy, especially if it is an office that takes on sensitive jobs. The boss can then keep an eye on who's coming and going. And even when he's not in his office, it can represent his presence. The downside is that the boss gets no privacy; this was on display that morning.

I signed the muster and said 'Good morning' to Saee at the reception. When she didn't reply, I saw her looking somewhere over my shoulder. I turned to see trouble brewing in Premendra's cabin. Swarupa and he were going at each other, hammer and tongs, standing up and shouting. Swarupa was pregnant. She was in her sixth month. I didn't have to be a doctor to know that she shouldn't be doing stuff like this. Dixit, in charge of liaison and follow-up, was next to her, his head down. Srinivas Pant, Senior Partner, Pant-Prabhu Associates, was sitting at the window, keying something in on his cell phone or at least pretending to. The glass was soundproof so nothing could be heard outside but it was clear that it was a storm.

Premendra turned in my direction and when he saw me, he fell silent, as if struck by lightning. Dixit and Pant followed the direction of his gaze and for the next two or three seconds, there was silence. Then Swarupa collapsed in a chair as if the strength had drained from her legs and began to sob. I ran to the cabin and knocked before entering. Everyone kept looking from me to Swarupa and back again but no one said anything. When I went up to Swarupa and put a hand on her shoulder, she jerked away. She looked at me for a moment and then without another word, she ran out of the room. I stood there looking after her foolishly.

~

Even remembering that moment brings a lump to my throat. Swarupa did not speak with me at all that day. Actually, after that we didn't speak much at all. Or you could say that the Swarupa I had known had vanished. From Premendra, I learned that she had felt betrayed, betrayed by me. Since she had been worried about me and had heard about Sushrut's asking for me to be excused from site visits, she had taken them on herself. The stress and the heat had apparently gotten to her. The doctors had told her there were complications with her pregnancy: the foetus was not growing satisfactorily. She should not have been working so hard. They were doing some tests but they advised complete bed rest.

'So?' I asked, worried.

'So nothing. We have to let her go.' Premendra said.

'*Arre baap re*, but she's worked so hard. And if the doctors have recommended bed rest what can she do?' I tried to fight her case.

'No need to take her side,' Premendra said quietly. 'You have no idea how badly she speaks of you. She feels you've wormed your way into my good books and sidelined her. God forbid, if she should have further health problems, she'll lay those at your doorstep too.'

So I had been left in the dark. If she had felt this way, why hadn't she ever spoken to me about it? Had I been really so wrapped up in my own troubles? So wrapped up as to be blind to what was going on in front of me?

Premendra had continued speaking: 'Practically speaking, I had no other way. In such a situation, it would have been impossible for you two to work together. So I was compelled to let one of you go. Right now what you're handling in terms of design coordination and follow up, is more important so the decision was easy. And she's been told to rest for a few months. It isn't just about her working here; it's also a discipline thing. She can't confront me like this. I am not her friend, I'm her boss. Tolerating this would be a bad precedent. I had no choice but to make an example.'

Premendra was as good as his word. Swarupa was made to resign that day. She still came to work during her notice period but she said very little to me. She handed over her work to the new hire, Parul Shah. Now all communication had ceased. I tried to talk to her, to confront her once or twice, but she had taken to looking at me in an entirely new way. Then one day she suddenly stopped coming. We got the news that she had been admitted to hospital. For a while after that, nothing. Then we heard that she had had to undergo a Caesarean section, one month early. A boy was born but so low in birth weight that his chances were doubted. He was kept under observation for a week or so, but he survived. Some of the staff went for the baby shower. I wasn't invited nor was Premendra. It took time for Swarupa to get back to normal. For a year or so, she was at home. And somewhere along the way, our friendship ended. There seemed no point in trying to start again.

~

Before replying to Swarupa, I phoned Sushrut. When he is not involved, Sushrut can see things clearly. Or so I have observed. But this time he was no use. The phone rang on and on. It seemed to be a sign: I would have to make my own call on this one. I took the hint. I picked up the phone, and keyed in '[_]>shop. Nxt 15 mts', pressed the 'Send' button, ordered coffee and settled down to wait.

I knew that in choosing me over Swarupa, Premendra had acted in his own interests. But I also knew that he had fallen in my eyes by making this decision. I could not keep my mind on the work. I knew that I had been cast as villain/vamp of the piece. And not long afterwards, I struck camp too. Although Agashe and Antya were three years my senior in college, we were good friends, we had kept in touch, with telephone calls at least. They were considering starting their own practice. And so SNA was formed. During these days and even afterwards, I kept hearing some dribs and drabs about Swarupa. In a year she was back, and soon afterwards she got funding for her own NGO. It was called SEVA but I hadn't bothered to find out the full form. A while later, she got divorced.

Presumably her television-star husband had been indulging in extracurricular activities as his wife got busy with her career. Swarupa was not the kind to take that lying down. I heard that she and her son—his name was Aavart or something fashionable like that—were now living somewhere in Kandivali. SEVA was doing very well, but because I was with SNA we got no work there. She would make vague statements about us—more specifically about me—that were difficult to prove or disprove. This seemed to be an unwritten policy with SEVA. I could understand her anger that I had been chosen over her but I found it odd that she could keep this bitterness going. Anyway, it was time for a confrontation. The signs were all there.

~

I thought I knew what she looked like—I'd seen pictures of her in the papers from time to time—but when she appeared in front of me, it took me a moment to recognize her. When we were friends, she had been a bit stout and didn't take much care of her appearance. But she made up for it with an almost childlike pleasantness, a happy-go-lucky manner. Her face made people want to help her. This was part of how she got things done. Perhaps it was the increasing responsibilities after the divorce or the custody battle that followed, but that childlike demeanour was gone. Her face was stern now, sharp. She was also thinner. Her clothes—Fab India chic—were so well chosen in their cut and colour that she could go from a gate meeting to a five-star hotel without stopping.

'Well, you haven't changed,' she said, as if nothing had happened between us.

I didn't find it that easy.

'Why did you SMS me?'

'I had work with you. Listen to me. And then curse if you want,' she said in a low voice. She had not lost her matter-of-fact way of talking. I had finished my coffee but I did want to listen.

'What work?' I felt my temper rising. She couldn't do this. For no fault of mine, she had pursued a vendetta against me. This must be a new strategy…'If you believe that I will just…'

She stopped me in the middle of the sentence. Perhaps my voice had been a little louder than necessary. I looked around. There were some other tables outside the coffee shop and they were occupied but no one seemed to be paying any attention to us.

'I took Aavart to Matunga yesterday. My uncle lives there.'

'I know,' I said, by reflex. I could have bitten my tongue.

'Oh yes. We stayed there once. I'd forgotten,' she said. 'Aavart is my son.'

I managed to stop myself from saying that I knew that too.

'When we left, it was eight. You never get parking there so I hadn't taken the car. And when do you ever get a cab when you need one? So I decided to walk and got to Khodadad Circle in Dadar. By then Aavart was hungry. I was too. As we were debating what to eat, I thought of the bhelwala. I hadn't been in those parts for quite a while. But luckily he was still there. He hadn't been sacrificed on the altar of redevelopment. Aavart was delighted. He fell to but I found that though I was hungry I didn't feel like eating anything. Memories of the old days were coming back. How we would leave office and go there afterwards. How well we got on. And then other things also came back…the mess in the office, the anger I felt…the years of hurt…all of it. Then I began to ask what the issue really was. Was there any substantial reason for me to be angry? With you, at any rate? When that anger began, there was a threat to Aavart's life. Should I have stayed angry after he was born and had pulled through splendidly? Or was it just the loss of my job, the illness, the divorce, one thing after another, that had left me angry with you? Was I trying to keep this anger alive so I would be able to blame someone else rather than taking responsibility? Looked at from that angle, was it all really so bad? Quitting SEHAT meant that I was forced to sink or swim. And when I began to swim, I ended up even more successful and that's a fact.

'I had not even thought about this because I'd stopped thinking about my past except with reference to you. When all these things came up I became uncomfortable. It was at that moment that I decided that I had to meet you. I got your number and had saved it but I didn't have the courage to take the next step. Then I saw you in the car and I thought: now or never.'

Swarupa stopped as if someone had stamped on the brakes. I didn't know what she expected. Did she think I'd get up and leave? Throw a fit? Tell her she had done no wrong?

For two minutes, I sat there quietly. Who had been in the wrong? She or me? Up till now I had never counted myself as blameless in the whole thing but now she was telling me her side of things, why was I getting angry? It was clear to me that if I were to even open my mouth, we would never be friends again.

I had to get away. I had to find some time, some space to think things through. Who was going to give that to me? There was nothing I could do, nothing I could say.

No matter where, you are as comfortable as you want to be. So I had always maintained. Now Swarupa had taken me out of my comfort zone and made me test my own beliefs.

When it was no longer possible to remain silent, I opened my mouth even though I didn't know what I was going to say. But just then Swarupa's phone rang and she got up. Lalvani had got a court order against the morcha. Police action was going to start against it. She had to return to her station. As she rushed off, she pushed a card into my hand and said: 'Please give me a call.'

For the next hour until Antya arrived, I continued to sit there. The missed calls and text messages on my phone (which was on silent mode) and the number of empty coffee mugs kept increasing. And yet my mind seemed oddly at peace, as if a critical moment had passed.

'Sushrut is desperately trying to call you,' Antya said. 'Why aren't you picking up your phone?'

'Sorry, I didn't realize. I'll call him,' I said. 'Shall we go?'

'Yes, I think I've met everyone and you don't look like you can schmooze any more,' Antya said, wiping the lenses of his spectacles. 'So I guess we're done.'

I laughed and picked up my purse.

'So what was Swarupa saying?' he asked carefully.

'She said the bhelwala at Khodadad Circle still makes a mean ragda puri,' I said, and getting out of the chair, walked away, giving him no opportunity to reply.

I felt as if I had put down a burden I had been carrying for years. The day had not been wasted after all and there was all night for celebrations.

SUBMISSION

As I looked at the study model rocking slowly in time with the motion of the train, I realized that I did not know the exact term for the iron bracket on which it was resting. Could it be 'carrier'? That's what you'd find on the back of a bicycle. Both hold up stuff and are made of roughly the same material; nothing else in common. But if you don't know, it's as good a name as any. After all, both of them carry things, right?

Then the local train hit the brakes abruptly and we all lurched against each other. The train squeaked and squealed to a halt. I grabbed hold of the iron grip of a seat—what is that called?—to keep myself from falling. I ground out a Marathi cuss word.

To express true outrage you need a bhasha. These English ones seem a bit weak, and how many variations can you have on the single word 'Fuck'?

From my spot, I extended a hand and made sure the model was safe and then looked at my watch. The other people in the train were also getting restless.

All those who could were leaning out of the train to see what was going on. But there was nothing really to be seen. With a grunt, we began to move again. This time I was braced and ready. I did not think I was going to make it in time to college today. Today was the first major submission of the design thesis, ninth semester, and naturally the day my car decided not to start. It's a new car, not even a year old, and already it's giving me trouble.

I should bloody sue Honda for this. I should tell Dad to find out about the procedures for filing a complaint in the consumer courts.

But until then there was nothing to do but to get into a crowded train with the model on which my career depended, and squeeze into the fourth seat which fell vacant only at Mahalaxmi Station. From my point of view, having this model when I'm being marked is very important. It's not that I think I won't be able to explain my design but I am not sure that my concept will be clear. After all, it is not a question of one or two buildings; I'm proposing a revolutionary alternative for downtown Mumbai. In other words, a neighbourhood restructuring with heritage structures, traffic alternatives, multi-layered functionality...all of the above. I didn't think drawings alone would explain what I was proposing. My guide, Kanvinde, is a sensible sort. He's not completely decrepit yet, so he gets our way of thinking but I'm not sure he sees my point of view. In his opinion, I should have taken an easier subject but I have put in too much work to change now. And why should I take an easy subject? When I pass out I'll have to do whatever work I get, right? So why can't I do stuff that I really want to do now when I'm still in college? Actually that's only the superficial explanation.

In truth, my nature is like that.

Once I decide, I hate to change my mind. And so, once I had decided to do my thesis on Mumbai Urban Planning, nothing and nobody was going to make me choose something else. Even if the dean had asked me I would have not changed my topic. And anyway, I wouldn't listen to Kanvinde. Not now. Ever since I found out about him and Riddhima, he has fallen in my esteem somewhat.

When there was some room to move, the first thing I did was to take my phone out of my trouser pocket and call Dad. He was in a meeting but no worries. He always takes my calls. I don't waste his time either. I told him about the problem with the car and he said he'd send his driver to take the car to the dealer. The next call I made was to Riddhima.

'Hi Harsh, how's everything?'

The voice wasn't Riddhima's and behind it the sound of laughter.

'Who's this?' I said, trying to decipher the identity of the person in the clamour of the train and all the people around. Really, I should get Dad to buy one of those Bose hands-free sets with noise reduction…then these things won't happen. On the other hand, I don't travel in trains so much, do I?

'You don't recognize my voice? I am so hurt, Harsh.'

More giggles. Then: 'Saumya here!'

Saumya. Riddhima's little sister.

Naturally.

'Hey Saumya. No school today?' I tried to put the right degree of irony into my voice. 'Where's Riddhima? When will she reach college?'

'She's driving. All of us are coming today. You've got some presentation, na? That's why. She has some huge sheets and we're doing coolie-giri. I bunked school. Rohan's here too. You know Rohan, na?'

'Of course I know Rohan. The one from your building, right?'

Actually I knew Rohan and not just as my friend's sister's friend. Rohan is the son of the architect Anant Redij, and Redij is one of the principal partners of a very young, very influential architectural firm in Mumbai. I've never met Anant Redij myself but I was hoping that Rohan would introduce me. His firm, SNA, was my best bet for a really worthwhile professional practice.

'Yup. The one and only,' Saumya shrieked into my ears. 'We'll reach in about fifteen minutes. Riddhima is asking if you've reached already.'

'On my way.'

Before Saumya could make any further inquiries I ended the call and tried to figure out which station was coming next, but I'd be damned if I could see through the crush of people. A young man had taken up residence against the window. He was about my age and had struck a rather macho body-building sort of pose there.

He was wearing a T-shirt with short sleeves and was strap-hanging in a way that was meant to show off his muscles. As if that wasn't enough, a short girl had wound her arms around his waist and was holding on tight. She was probably using the excuse of her shortness to explain why she was holding on to her boyfriend instead of a strap. I really dislike people like that on principle.

Look at them now. Their romance is blocking my view. I tried to get another look out of the train but the hero-type began to wonder what I was looking at.

He shifted his eyes and swelled up his biceps and began to look daggers at me. So I sat back quietly. I had no desire to become the subject of a display of his strength.

What I do not understand is why women insist on travelling in the general compartments at peak hours. So this one's boyfriend is a muscular ape who can take care of her. But what about the poor men who have almost no place to stand? If you must make this public display of affection, aren't there gardens or multiplexes enough for that kind of thing? But no. I began to curse—ripe bhasha curses—when suddenly the train began to slow down and Short-and-Sweet and Mr Muscles moved from the window and I could look out. The area seemed familiar now so I began to make preparations to descend. Mental preparations, that is. People drop easily off running trains at Churchgate but I had a model to carry. The campus is far enough to make walking a pain but close enough to make getting a taxi difficult. If Ramya were with me, he would have told the taxi-driver that he wanted to go somewhere far off—Byculla, say—and then at the college, he'd ask him to stop for a moment and get off. But that's not me. I don't like being on the receiving end of justifiable abuse from taxi-drivers or anyone of that class. Or to be more correct, I don't want to be on the receiving end of any kind of abuse. Ramya doesn't care. It's not for nothing that Riddhi says he has the hide of a rhino.

As I said, Riddhima is Riddhi. Ramya is Ramakant. And me. That's my group. Actually it surprises me. Because Ramya is not the sort of person to be included in any sort of group. Perhaps we tolerate him because he was in school with me and because Riddhi was in love with him for a couple of years.

Now, why she should love him, I wouldn't know. I have never seen him encouraging her. Outside his work, his on-going fight with his father and the cigarettes that dangle from his lips for ten to fourteen hours a day (depending, of course, on college hours), he shows no interest in anything else.

His father's various affairs—in every sense of the word—and his being the only child mean that he has no money worries. You'd think he'd make some adjustments for the sake of money. But if he did, would he be Ramya? Last year, he fought with his father and left the house. His parents were already divorced. But his mother is somewhere abroad—Australia, I think—so he'd stayed with me for a month but how long could my folks take his smoking and general bad behaviour? Fortunately, after a month he and his father came to some sort of an agreement and he was given a separate apartment to stay. Every month, his old man would put fifty thousand into his account. Ramya would blow up about twenty thousand, mainly on cigarettes. The rest would just sit there. This balance kept growing. He had no other connection with his father other than this economic one.

I knew about his messy family life so he was comfortable with me; and since Riddhi was my friend, by extension, with her as well. He didn't care that she cared but then he doesn't care about much. As for Riddhi, she likes Ramya but she trusts me more.

And so when Kanvinde began his pursuit and started saying suggestive things to Riddhi, I was the first to hear about it. It's another thing that I was the one who told Ramya about it. Ramya doesn't like anyone else in class. This is because he's totally antisocial, except for us. He speaks to no one. Everyone hates him but the teachers love him, because he's practically a genius. He doesn't care much for history, but in every other subject, he makes everyone look bad just by being present. So none of the students like him and since he's our friend, by extension, everyone keeps their distance from us—which actually doesn't bother me that much—but it means we're kind of stuck with each other.

Though it's time for college to begin, it's difficult to say when Ramya is going to show up with one of his freehand sketches of something so ingenious and fundamental that he just has to get the best grades.

His basic belief is that laws are made for other people and do not apply to him. So it was a bit of a shock to see him outside the college—on time.

He was taking his last few drags before entering the college and talking to Riddhima outside the gate. He had the blue backpack he had bought for himself when his old man had taken him to Japan; and as always, a roll of tracings was sticking out of it.

And yet in the moment that I looked at him I knew that something was different. The weeks-at-a-time jeans, slit at the knee with a blade, had been replaced by a pair of black trousers; the faded T-shirt by a blue Van Heusen shirt. It would have been difficult for him to part and tame his hair but it had been cropped short. He had even shaved.

The change was radical. Something was wrong.

Not far off, Riddhima's Swift, parked any old how, and Saumya and Rohan were standing outside it, chatting. I took myself over.

'Hey guys, how's it going?' I asked, setting my model down on the top of the Swift. We were late already but since it was individual interaction day, five or ten minutes this way or that would make no difference. And Riddhi from my group was right here so she was going to be late too. I thought I'd chat with the kids and do a little PR too. But Rohan seemed different. He seemed very quiet. Saumya was herself, burbling and laughing.

I even said to her: 'Rohan doesn't seem to be in the

mood to talk,' and that quietened her a little. Then she said, 'Nothing of the kind, he's always like that. Forget him.'

At this Rohan looked at her and then turned away to look at the spreading banyan trees of our campus. I didn't push it. You could see he was not in the mood to chat. Some personal shit, maybe.

I was about to leave when Riddhi arrived.

'What are you doing here? Don't you want to go to class?'

'Just got here. I saw these two and stopped. What's with him?' I indicated Ramya's new look.

'Aah. You'd better ask him,' she said. 'Parents. Can't live with them, can't live without.'

She suppressed a smile and slapped Rohan on the back and winked at Saumya.

I didn't get it but Saumya obviously did. Because she laughed loudly. Rohan kept looking at Riddhi. All this was going over my head.

'Go on ahead. I'll come with Ramya,' I said.

'Suit yourself,' she said, opening the trunk of the car and took out some drawing sheets. I picked up my model and left. Ramya was still lost in his own thoughts and was trying to get the last drags of his ciggie.

'Hey genius,' I said, 'what's Riddhima saying?'

'How would I know?' He said, throwing away the stub. It hit Shyamal Verma's portfolio. Shyamal stopped in his tracks.

'Sorry, my bad,' Ramya drawled, raising his hands in

mock surrender. Shyamal gave him a look and turned and walked off, saying nothing. No one wanted to cross Ramya. Perks of being weird I guess.

'She said something about parents?'

'Oh, that?'

'Yes, that.'

'My mother, man. She's coming back,' he said.

'Back as in?'

'As in, coming home. I think it's some ploy to get me to go back home.'

I was shocked. Good news, of course. The kind you'd celebrate. And all Ramya could do was turn this into something about him? Is there any limit to human self-centredness? I was about to lose it with him. But just then, the dean's car entered the campus and we thought it wise to make tracks.

'She's flying in this afternoon. It has been made mandatory for me to go to the airport and receive her,' he said, scraping his hands through his cropped hair.

'Crap,' I was about to laugh. 'So that's why you've gone respectable.'

'Yeah, go ahead, laugh all you want. See if I care. Anyway, I'm off,' Ramya said. 'I'm not staying for the lectures today. I just came because I needed some input on my projects. Got those. So I'll kill some time at the Café Coffee Day near Churchgate and sketch the rest. Then the airport.'

He gave me no opportunity to reply before walking away.

'Arre, whose inputs did you want?' I called after him but he was already some distance away. He vanished behind the parking lot wall. He might not even have heard.

Ten more minutes had passed by the time I got to class.

~

Our college is a big one. Each discipline has its own independent building—all spread out in the spacious grounds, each at some distance from the other. In general, this is very nice but when you have to carry a model and plod from one building to the next, it's a pain. Of course, there's an easy option. Get a junior to be your beast of burden. That's what I did. Parimal Chaturvedi (third semester) was reading a paperback outside the canteen. I pressed him into service and followed him, at my ease. Of course, my laptop bag was still on my shoulders but that's not much of a burden. I sometimes think that if I put it down, I might simply float away. It keeps me grounded.

I was about half an hour late for the 10 a.m. lecture. Counting me and Riddhi, there are ten of us in the group. Each person gets about ten to fifteen minutes of discussion time, at a pinch.

Since today was marking, I expected everyone to be present. I thought there'd be about seven or eight students in the class. So I was quite startled to see only two there. Riddhi was not one of them. How was that possible? She had gone ahead, at least ten minutes before me. And however mad about her he was, Kanvinde could not have possibly put all the others aside and taken her work first. She should have been around but she was nowhere in sight.

Chaturvedi set my model down with a little more force than was strictly necessary and Kanvinde looked up. Did a thin line spring up on his forehead? Or was it an illusion? But then without a word, he turned back to Sanjiv Shah who was sitting in front of him and began to discuss his drawings in a quiet voice.

That was Kanvinde's style. He never raised his voice. There were enough professors who roared and shouted and provided us with dramatics about delivering good work or bringing it in on time. Kanvinde did none of this. And so the students liked him a bit more. Even with an idiot like Sanjiv in front of him, he was speaking quietly. How much Kanvinde believes in what he is saying is a different issue. But you never feel that Kanvinde is rescuing you from your own idiocy. He manages to convince you that he respects your work. He makes you think he believes you will be able to do something, some day. I never bought into this act but many were fooled by it—and it *was* an act even if an effective one. Actually, even Riddhi didn't bother to separate what was true from what was false in his comments but accepted them blindly. But really Kanvinde was not just making comments about her designs. How could he do that? I was getting angry. No sign of Riddhi. Nor Rohan nor Saumya. Where could they be?

I could tell from his body language that Kanvinde was in no hurry to get to me. He was totally relaxed. I knew the level at which Sanju's designs operated. Even he would be surprised to discover that there was so much to discuss in them. But Kanvinde made no sign of releasing him. I tried to call Riddhi's cell but it was switched off. I unpacked my model and took out the bundle of drawings inside. I took out a paper and sat sketching, peacefully.

Finally, the Shahnama ended and I rose to my feet; but Kanvinde made a gesture to stop me and called Shreya Jaiswal. Properly speaking, I should have gone next in roll-number order but who was to tell him that? Perhaps Kanvinde felt my design was complicated and so he'd deal with it last. But he had never put me last before. Still what other reason could there be? And we hadn't had a row for him to be taking revenge. It wasn't as if I took all his advice; but then no one did. No one was expected to. They're teachers, not bosses. Some leeway is available.

Sanju moved his stuff and as he left, signalled me to come out too. What could he want with me? But when things start going wrong, they just keep on going wrong. Outside, Sanju was leaning on the wall and looking at the crowds in front of the canteen.

'What's up with Riddhima?' Sanju asked, shoving his spectacles up on his nose.

'What is?'

'I don't know Harsh, you tell me.'

'Tell you about what? What's going on?'

'She was crying.'

'Crying? Riddhima? Why?' I was shocked.

'How do I know? When she came in with her stooges, marking had already started,' Sanju said. 'I think Rohit was already down and then Susham…or was it…'

'Sanju, why was she crying?' I began to get irritated.

'I don't know but I'll tell you what happened.'

'Please. But make it quick. I'm up next.' I said, trying to hide my annoyance.

'Okay. When she came, someone was being marked. Kanvinde saw her and finished it up. Then he said he was going to postpone today's marking because no one's work amounted to much. He was also in a hurry. An urgent meeting or something. So if anyone had anything important, they should wait. The rest hopped it. Shreya and I stayed. And Riddhima, of course. Then he called her.'

This was something new. That today was marking-day had been decided earlier. Now a change of plan. None of which explained why Riddhima was crying. I looked at Sanju, still puzzled. But he didn't know what had really happened. Despite being on the second bench.

'Honestly, Harsh, I couldn't hear a thing. Anyway, I was sorting out my notes. And they were speaking really softly. Not even for long. Four or five minutes perhaps. Then the chair scraped back loudly so I looked up. Riddhi was standing. She spun around and ran out. I could see she was crying. And those guys with her? They were on the last bench, they ran after her. That's all I know.'

'You mean Riddhi was upset because Kanvinde didn't like her designs?'

I tried to apply the simplest possible explanation to the matter.

But Sanju was not inclined to help.

'I don't mean to say anything,' he said quietly. 'I'm telling you what happened. You figure out what it means. But if you ask me, it was something personal.'

'Personal?'

To which he just shrugged and started packing up his stuff. I tried Riddhi's phone again after he left. Still switched off.

I went into class and sat down on the last bench. Something was wrong. Had Kanvinde threatened Riddhi because she wasn't playing along? She had all the answers but she wasn't around.

At one point, I thought I should leave.

But I had put a lot of work into lugging that model to class by train, no less, and I wasn't going to let that go to waste. I am stubborn enough for that.

When I put my model down in front of Kanvinde, my thoughts were somewhere else. But if Kanvinde was aware of this he gave no indication of it at all. He just moved it to the side and began to look at my drawings. I began to speak but he indicated that I should be silent. He began to tally the drawings and the model. Without saying so much as a word to me, he spent the next ten minutes comparing the model and the drawings. Finally, he set the drawings aside and looked at me. He took off his rimless glasses and took out a monogrammed handkerchief from his pocket.

'Good work. Your subject was a complicated one. I didn't think you'd be able to pull it off,' he said as he polished the lenses.

'Thank you, sir.' I said, with a sigh of relief.

For the next five minutes or so, he talked about the design. He had really got it. In fact so clearly that I began to wonder why I had wasted time with a study model. But no, it was all to the good. It had helped me clarify certain concepts to myself. In those five minutes, my mood changed so dramatically, I almost forgot about Riddhi.

And then he asked: 'Who told you I'm chasing Riddhima?'

'Sir?'

'It's an easy question and you know the answer.'

I said nothing. We'd been talking about these designs and urban infrastructure, so how had Riddhima suddenly got into the conversation?

'I know this for a fact, Harsh. She told you that I'm in love with her, that I make suggestive remarks, right? She tells you some rubbish and you go blabbering it to other people?'

'To others? Where did I…?'

'You know,' Kanvinde was in full flow. 'Reputation is an important thing. However intelligent a man is or however capable, it doesn't matter to most people. They think it's more important how good he is. Consider this: I know how bright you are. This work is proof. But this behaviour–does it become someone of your intelligence?'

For a moment, I couldn't believe my ears. He was threatening me, the son of a bitch.

'There's been a misunderstanding, sir,' my voice sounded hollow now. I wasn't prepared for a confrontation. And what kind of a confrontation? One person's word against another. Who was right? Who was wrong? How was one to know? It was 'he said-she said'. I began to feel claustrophobic. The tubelight above the window began to crackle loudly.

'Perhaps it isn't your fault. Riddhima told you and you believed her blindly. But does it sound right to you? That I would do this to a student? I've taught at this college for seven years. I have some reputation. Do you know what havoc your thoughtlessness might wreak upon it?'

'Sir, I said nothing to anyone,' I tried a last appeal.

'I do not wish to argue with you. You are intelligent enough to know what you must do. And do not think I am threatening you. I have no intention of failing you or anything like that. Riddhima is a fool but I will not fail her either. I just explained her foolishness to her. This matter is closed. I will not say another word about it. But it was my duty to tell you that I know what you have done. I want this stopped immediately.'

Bastard! In my anger, I couldn't even think of a good Marathi expletive.

As if Kanvinde was doing us a favour by not failing us. And he'd added that disclaimer that he wasn't going to fail us so I couldn't report him. It was wrong on his part to try and take advantage of his students. As I walked down the stairs, I was wondering where Riddhima was and what state her head was in. And there was rage against Ramya.

Because, other than me, the only other person who knew was Ramya.

Was that why he'd got here early?

After that day, I never got a chance to talk properly to Riddhi again. She'd left with Saumya and Rohan before I got down the stairs. For the next month, she refused to talk to me, other than just banal conversation. The next semester, she joined Rohan's dad's firm for professional training. Because of the awkwardness between us, I did not apply there. But I confronted Ramya that very day. After all, I knew where he was going to be.

~

He was at the CCD in front of Churchgate Station, slugging coffee and sketching. As always, he was sitting outside. CCD doesn't allow people to smoke but if there are no crowds, they ignore Ramya's cigarette. The tips he leaves help. But he wasn't smoking, though there were a few stuffed into a packet on the table. He still had ten or fifteen minutes before he had to leave for the airport.

'Sit,' he said and called, 'Boss, one vegan shake.'

When I saw how cool he was, all the carefully prepared sentences evaporated. Had this guy ever cared about anyone's responses that he might feel something now that I was feeling bad? Would it matter to him that Riddhi had been humiliated in class? Whoever said, 'No man is an island,' had not met Ramya. He was truly an island: independent; self-created. We might think that our behaviour, our friendship, our presence or absence might mean something to him but it didn't. Not that day. Not now.

Still, I did ask for an explanation.

'You told Kanvinde about Riddhi?'

He laughed and said, 'Indeed. Who else knows?' and he calmly took a cigarette from the packet and lit it.

'Why?' I couldn't bear his calmness. This man calls himself our friend and then…

And then a thought struck me. He didn't call himself our friend. He hung out with us. Had we misunderstood that?

'There was no other way,' he said, putting the cigarette carefully down on the edge of the pack.

'For what?' I didn't understand.

'To get rid of Riddhi.'

'Means?'

'Easy. You know what she felt about me?'

'Yes. She is…actually she *was* in love with you.'

'Well, I wasn't in love with her. She's nice like that but what does that prove? Eventually, I've got to think of myself,' he said, picking up the cigarette again. 'You should know this: I have no belief left in relationships. Perhaps I never did. I tried to tell her that so many times but, man, she was totally deaf. You wouldn't believe how many discussions we've had over this one subject in the past month.'

Would I not believe? How could I believe or not believe when they'd been careful to tell me nothing? Not him, not Riddhi. How could she have found so many trivial things to talk to me about, when her relation with Ramya was at such a critical juncture?

'Finally I decided I had to find a way to hurt her so badly that she wouldn't come near me again. Perhaps not near you, either. But don't worry, Kanvinde won't fail you. He promised me.'

The coffee arrived. I pushed it aside and said to him, 'But why drag me into it? You could have told Kanvinde that she told you.'

'You have no sense of drama, Harsh. I needed to create the effect of a rumour that was spreading. He might not even have brought it up with her if I had let him believe that it was just me she had told,' Ramya seemed delighted with his smarts. 'This way it all worked out.'

'Worked out?'

I looked down and put my head into my hands. Why had he done it? Because his island status had been challenged? Or had his mother's return been the last straw, something that had shown him the shallowness in relationships? Even though he had explained, I was lost. He could have told me his problem. I could have talked to Riddhi. This was the equivalent of using a machine gun to kill a cockroach.

'You look hurt,' he said and raised an eyebrow at me. 'You aren't in love with her in the way she's in love with me, are you?'

And much amused by his own joke, he dropped some money on the counter and sauntered off to meet his mother.

I sat there for a long time. I had no reply for the question he had asked in jest. But I began to have some glimmerings of the answer—even as the certainty grew that there was no point knowing.

FAIR

IT RAINED THAT DAY, ON AND OFF AND ON AGAIN. JULY, so I wasn't surprised. Even before the school's yellow air-conditioned bus passed Parsi Colony, I was thinking up a lie I could try out on Aai. Though I don't know why I should. I'm not the kind of person to tear my clothes or dirty them up. And should that be something to get upset about, dirtying clothes? After all haven't the ads been screaming '*Daag achchhe hain*' into the ears of all and sundry? Hasn't penetrated their heads, has it? Even though they spend hours in front of the television watching interminable Marathi television serials they learn nothing. How can they? The ads mean work time: from cooking to lectures about homework to their kids, they fit it all into the commercial breaks. I don't know how anyone can watch one of those serials. I can't stand them. Why can't the whole blinking lot turn out one good serial among them? Just learn from American programming, na? I only watch downloaded American serials. But hold on…that's not the point.

We were talking about my clothes. Granted I'm not very neat in a general manner of speaking, but it isn't as if

I roll in the dirt every day. But the last few days have been bad. Specially ever since I stole the pen drive with Sunny Leone on it from Jello and took it to the Counsellor's cabin, those three have been after me. 'Those three' means Mahadik's gang: Mahadik, Jello and Sant. Now I didn't mean to frame them. Why would I want to?

But we were tired of listening to Counsellor Smith's non-stop speeches on behavioural patterns. 'We' means me and Pushy aka Pushkar. So I thought I'd show him that if he had so many problems with us not studying he ought to see what the other students were up to. Don't get me wrong. It isn't as if we're some holy Joes either. Think about it—when the internet and Wi-Fi have made things so easy, it would be stupid not to do some additional research, right? But we don't bring that stuff to school. I mean, how stupid is that? And I'm not a kid anymore, am I? I mean, I'll be going to the ninth next year. Well, hopefully.

So when Jello, Mahadik and Sant were looking at something on a Netbook during the long break, I noticed. When they went to the playground, I lifted Jello's pen drive. I wrote their names on a piece of paper and left it with the pen drive in Counsellor Smith's cabin. I was about to hook off when Principal Mehta came out of his cabin. From Jello to Pushy, we were all hauled up to the Principal's office and our parents were called.

I got it in the neck too. I got a whole bunch of lectures from Dad. My internet access was cut off for a month, except for work on assignments which I had to do in the living room under my mother's eye. As if that stuff had been found on my pen drive! But who's to tell these guys? As if that wasn't enough, the parents of my group—Saumya's, Pushkar's and Bhavin's parents—were taken aside and told how I'm a bad influence and how they should keep their kids away from me. Bhavin is a scholar and Saumya lives in our building. Even Pushy is all right. All their parents have known me for some time now and they know I'm okay. When the Principal was talking in this serious voice, I wanted to laugh. This is one of my worst habits. If someone is saying something very seriously or someone is telling a sob story or even sometimes at funerals, I get the giggles. I have to dig my nails into my thighs or pinch myself hard. Then it fades a bit. Anyway, that day I managed not to laugh.

But Dad wasn't too happy about the whole episode. Actually, he was planning to go to the US for six to seven months to set up a project his firm had got with the Rednecks Group. I was hoping that by the time he got back, he would have forgotten but now I hear that he's got Sanika Aunty to go instead of him. That means we're all up shit creek again.

Anyway, ever since that day Jello, Sant and Mahadik have been after us. Not just me and Pushy but Bhavin too, just because he's our friend. Saumya escaped because she is a girl and I think Mahadik has a thing for her. Anyway, the three of us get the usual threats: 'Meet me outside. See what I'll do to you.' And since I took the pen drive, I get the worst of it. Mahadik gets me alone and throws ink on my clothes, pushes me about during the break. He's quite strong so the other kids are afraid of him. Up to now I haven't hit back. But what about my clothes? By the time I get home, they are a mess and I get blamed since I'm not the kind to rat on anybody. And after this problem with the Principal, I don't want this thing to drag out. So every day I invent a new story about my clothes and hope that Aai will believe it. I don't think today's shirt can be used again. Like it's totally ripped. Torn into two. Through the day, I managed to keep the three of them at a distance. But in the last period, everything went haywire. The rain had just stopped and the ground was full of slush. When we went for physical training, Mayuresh Sir decided that we should do some football practice and I ended up in the team against those three. They did everything they could to get me. By the end of practice my shirt was a total wreck and my knees were also scraped. I got the school nurse to bandage my knees, took a tetanus shot, borrowed a T-shirt from Bhavin's locker and ran to get the school bus.

In the bus I met Saumya and for the next twenty minutes we shot the breeze. I say that Saumya is part of my group and the teacher folk also think so. But this isn't the entire truth. Like we're good friends and for the last few years we've been in the same division. But this year her division is different and her style too, and even though we both live in the same building and we always meet in the school bus, she does not mix with us as freely as she used to. A couple of months ago, she had told me about her crush on Bhavin, but if she had a crush on Bhavin, it would be logical for her to be with us, right? But if she were logical she wouldn't be Saumya, would she? She's found some chamchas in her class and every long break she holds a durbar on the first-floor corridor near the cooler.

The durbar means Ami and Vedant as chamchas and Shreya, her friend from her division. She and Shreya sit on the parapet and gossip about the boys while the chamchas hang around. Secretly they wanted to line maaro Saumya. Let the losers try! That way she's good looking. Lots of guys have tried. Before Mahadik decided to take me down, he would suck up to me hoping I'd help him get in good with her. That's my job in life, right? To help Mahadik with his love life!

Before our stop came it had warmed up a little and my legs weren't hurting so much. Saumya advised, tell Aai the truth—but on the phone before reaching home, with some additional drama. This would mean that she would be more concerned about the injury than my clothes. I could see the point. I took out my phone and was about to call when I thought, 'Forget it. Let her say what she wants but let her say it after fifteen minutes. At least now I can sit quiet.'

When I got off the bus it was raining again. I hate the rain. Like it's all right if I'm in school or at home or in any other dry place. I have no objection to it raining outside when I'm dry but otherwise, yuck. What I hate most? When you wear shorts and muck splashes the backs of your legs. You can't see it properly, you can't clean it properly and you have to walk slowly, placing each foot fully on the ground. You can't even think about running. How poets can write things about the rains, I don't know. They all must be sitting at home with the windows firmly closed and a pile of stationery at their elbows.

So anyway, I got off the bus under Saumya's umbrella.

I don't like carrying umbrellas. I have to keep track of them and however much I try, they get lost. When Saumya is around, I don't have a problem. In these matters, she's very reliable. Only, you can't let her know that that's why you need her.

'Why the crowds?' Saumya asked.

'Crowds? What crowds?' I looked around for the first time. I'm like that. I see what I want to see. I don't see anything else. I just don't pay attention. It's like I'm a horse with blinkers on. I think they're in-built. Like, if I'm thinking about something or looking at something, I can't think about something else, I can't see anything else. Sometimes I don't even hear when people call me. Everyone thinks I'm doing it on purpose. Or I'm rude.

So at that point, all I was thinking of was what lie I should tell Aai and how. This meant I was in blinker mode and other than Saumya and our building gate, I was seeing nothing else. But when she mentioned crowds, I did notice that there were more people around than usual. There were piles of plastic sheets and bamboo poles stacked against the walls of the compound. Two or three people were marking the ground near our gate with the white oil paint they were scraping out of small cans of dryish paint, even as they huddled under tattered umbrellas.

When we had left for school nothing of this was happening. Now it seemed as if a battalion had arrived. But once you realized why they were there, their presence was no surprise. If you ask me, anyone who lives on this road has no business asking why there are crowds, especially in July. But Saumya is an exception. She can ask anything she wants.

'What do you mean why are there crowds? It's the jatra. I think it's day after tomorrow,' I said. Ten minutes' walking distance from where we live is a famous Vitthal Mandir. There's a jatra—an annual fair—every Ashad. It's a proper festival with lots of singing and chanting. This means food and drink stalls, games of skill, loud Marathi music and sometimes Hindi music too, soap bubbles randomly bobbing about, sugarcane bundles, a giant wheel and lots of people. So many people in fact that it reminds you of those old Hindi films where kids routinely get lost at the mela. It took the city-ness out of the city. Trust me, it's crazy and chaotic...not to mention, absurd. That one should have a jatra like this, a village festival really, in the middle of a major metro like Mumbai which wants to compete with Hong Kong and New York, is unbelievable.

'Oh, what fun!' Saumya squeaked.

'Fun? It's a bore!'

'Arre, it's a religious thing.'

'What's religious about it? Hardly anyone comes for darshan. They want to buy those weird feather caps or the wooden whistles and don't even talk about the traffic. Even our bus won't be able to come in. We'll have to walk through crowds right up to the corner. You know, Teredesai's car got stolen during the jatra. Late in the night. It's not safe.'

'Every year you tell me this. I've heard it fifty times but I don't even know if it's true. I don't remember anything like that happening.'

'Forget it.' I left the protection of her umbrella and plunged into the rain towards the lobby. Saumya let me go. She walked slowly behind me.

That day when I came down to play I was still thinking about the jatra. In the evening, we meet quite late. That's because Pushy comes back from tuition only by 6:30. By that time Saumya has her singing class. (Don't ask!) I don't go to any classes or tuitions. So I generally use this time to hang out on Facebook. But with my net access cut off, that's out of the question. While I was pretending to listen to Aai's lecture, I updated my status on the phone. Two minutes later Dad posted an angry emoticon. I ignored it. One thing I don't get: these people keep saying they are very busy. Just yesterday he said he would be spending the whole day in an architectural seminar. So where does he get the time to check my status updates?

I logged out. I saw it had stopped raining. I came

down and took a short spin on my cycle. The markings on the footpath were complete but the stalls had not been built.

That would happen tomorrow and the commotion would begin that night and carry on until the next night. Dad was saying that when he was in school, the fair was much bigger than it is now. Who knows how they tolerated it? Maybe it was their timepass then. At that time, they say, TV was even sadder than it is now.

If Bhavin lived a little closer, it would have been nice. Like me, he doesn't go to any classes but for different reasons entirely. He's a scholar type, right? I don't go because I can't be bothered. Thinking about him brought Saumya to mind and made me grin. A crush! Saumya doesn't even know him.

Bhavin came to our school last year from Delhi. His father had been a client of SNA, so our dads are old pals. Dad suggested my school. In the whole of the last year, Bhavin must have said not more than four sentences to her. But we became good friends. When his family went to Delhi for a wedding, he was with us for eight days and the Saumya stuff happened. When I told Bhavin what Saumya had said, he laughed madly. '*Pagal hai woh*,' he said. She's mad.

~

By the time I had inspected the preparations for the jatra, Saumya's car and Pushy's cycle had returned from their respective classes. The arrangements to maintain queues at the temple, the building of the giant wheel in the gully at the back, the roadblocks the police had planned to set up…at least now it all looked organized. But trust me, systems always fail. Once crowds gather, things fall apart. When the pressure builds up, how are you going to keep things going, hold it all together? It takes just one crack and system failure begins, right? And then chaos. When Dad explained chaos theory, I totally loved it. It's like, totally natural. Systems are artificial, chaos is natural.

I was lounging on the lawn when Pushy cycled up and put his machine down. Meanwhile, Saumya got out of the car and the driver took it away to park it.

'So. Rohi, what's the jatra plan?' Pushy asked.

'Plan? I suppose we can hang out.'

'Anyway, it's so noisy that day, you can hardly do anything here,' Saumya said. 'Shall we call Bhavin?'

'Yeah. Right,' I said and looked at Pushy and laughed.

'Why Rohan?' Saumya got annoyed. 'What's it to you if he comes too? You're always on about what a great guy he is.'

'That's different and you know it,' I said. But there was no point taking it further. I just smiled.

Another idea was beginning to form. The cycling had started my knees hurting again. And I was thinking about my school foes.

'Listen,' I said slowly, eating up footage. 'What if we call Jello and Mahadik and Sant to the jatra?'

'Are you fucking nuts?' Saumya asked. She likes to use these hard-core cuss words when she's mad. Her elder sister studies architecture at the JJ School and she's her role model.

'Language, language!' said Pushy. 'This must be Rohan's bad influence showing up on you.'

'Hold on,' I said quietly, as if explaining things. 'Look, they give us shit, right? Do they or do they not?'

'They give *you* that,' Saumya was in no mood to listen.

'Saumya, let's listen to what he's saying,' Pushy said. 'It's not as if we're going to call them right now.' Then he turned to me, 'Rohan, they do make life miserable. And ever since your pen drive stunt, they're targetting us as well.'

'Correct. We can't do anything to them in school. But if they come here, it's open season on them.' I looked at Saumya and winked. She had her head down and had her beloved iPhone out.

'You want to beat them? And they're going to sit there and take it?' Pushy asked, disbelieving.

'No, but here we have the upper hand. Those three—no, those two actually—Jello is a blob. Not much use in a dust-up. And this is our area. There'll be crowds. If we do something in school, the peons or the teachers will come a-running. Who's to say anything here? They won't be able to complain in school either. The teachers won't believe it. And if people find out they got it from us, we just deny everything.'

'Too hypothetical,' Saumya began her objections. 'And what do you think, Rohan? You're going to call them and they'll come? Dimwit.'

'I agree with Saumya,' said Pushy. 'Won't they be suspicious?'

I looked from one to the other.

'I'm not saying we should invite them,' I said. Both looked at each other. I continued, 'We just call Bhavin. No, we don't call Bhavin. Saumya tells him to come alone. By letter. For a rendezvous. But we get the letter into Mahadik's hands. That will bring Mahadik here. They won't let the chance slip. To take revenge when Bhavin's alone. See if they don't. I'd bet on it. And then we teach them a lesson they won't forget.'

Three-second pause. You could have timed it. Then both began to speak at once.

~

Dad had just got home when I arrived at 9 p.m. Aai had probably been complaining about me. I heard bits and pieces: '…bad company…discipline…but you have to pay some attention.' I slipped into my room, set my iPod to full volume, chose the title track of *Skyfall* and stuck my head into a book. The evening meeting had gone well. Saumya and Pushy were on board. A tentative plan was in place. We talked to Bhavin too. As usual, he was all, 'No, yaar' and other mumble-grumbles but we kept at it until he agreed too.

It was a simple plan. Saumya was to type a love letter to Bhavin, complete with smileys and hearts and suchlike. Of course, Saumya can't be trusted to pull this off. I'm going to have to check that in the morning. She's supposed to call him to a quiet nook behind the temple via the letter. And then, as conspicuously as possible, she is to send me this letter via one of her chamchas. Why should a letter to Bhavin be sent to me? Because Mahadik's gang torments me. It would not be much use getting it to Bhavin. I had noticed that the Mahadik gang had been taking up strategic locations to keep an eye on Saumya and her durbar. This would ensure that the Mahadik gang would get to know Saumya had sent me a letter. They would certainly try and get hold of it if only to get something with which to mock me. I would, of course, surrender the letter. Mahadik's response would determine what we did at the jatra.

When I took my head out of the book, Dad was at the door, looking at me. He came in cautiously. He took the clothes off the beanbag and set them aside. Then he plumped up the bag and moved it to what he thought was the proper place for it. Behind him came Aai and she went and leaned against my Angry Birds poster. I took out the earphones, wrapped the cords around the iPod and put it on the shelf above my PC. Both their faces were serious and I felt the laughter rise up again.

~

The next day, it was raining buckets so when I was leaving, I took the umbrella Aai handed me without saying a word. Dad was checking news sites on his iPad and drinking coffee. That's what he always does. He has a routine and he doesn't like disruptions. He doesn't get upset, not really. He just gets rid of what doesn't fit into his system and goes on as if that person or thing doesn't exist. Our newspaperman's late deliveries, for instance, bugged him. So he eliminated newspapers. Now the newspaperman's timings don't worry him because he doesn't read the papers any longer; he reads the news online. Aai reads the gossip columns and the film reviews and then tosses the newspapers in the raddhi. Dad saw me and waved. I said nothing and left.

The road was now full of bamboo frames. The shopkeepers were sitting under the tarpaulins with their stuff. By night, they would all be ready for the jatra.

I corrected Saumya's letter and told her to get it ready by the short break. Pushy was quiet. I didn't say much myself. Outside it was still coming down. If it went on like this, what would happen to the jatra?

Through the day, I couldn't pay much attention. In the short break, I sat in class. Pushy went to Saumya's class to watch over the matter of the letter. Everything was in place but I was still thinking about Dad's ultimatum of the night before.

'Look, Rohan,' he had said in his usual quiet way. 'I think I have given you enough rope. It's okay that you're not at the head of your class. Not that I'm thrilled about it, mind you. Maybe you can't help that but you don't seem to be even trying. There have been complaints about you from your teachers. What they say to the other parents! Take that porn thing that just went down. Okay, I know that pen drive wasn't yours. But why did you have to get involved? Now Aarti says you come home dirty every day and give her a new reason each time. She thinks you're up to some goondagiri at school. This can't go on.'

He looked at Aai who was standing in a corner, trying to shrink into herself, avoiding my eyes, and after a glance, was back at me, 'I'm going to give you another month to pull yourself together. After that, I've scoped out a boarding school near Pune. It's a high-end school so you won't suffer. But it will be nothing like home.'

~

'Rohan,' Pushy's voice startled me and for a moment I just stared at him.

'You all right?' he asked, worried.

'Want to cancel?' Bhavin put in.

There was still time to do that. If it went bad, Dad would not wait a month before he sent me to Pune. But that would be giving the Mahadik gang a free pass. What worse could happen?

'No cancelling, you 'fraidy cats,' I said more to convince myself than them. 'Bhavin, you're not to come down. Remember that: no coming down. *Hum dono hi jaayenge*.' Only Pushy and I were to go down, I reminded him.

Bhavin made one last-ditch attempt to abort the mission.

'This plan is no good, yaar,' he said. 'Who sends love letters in this day and age? If Saumya wanted to call me somewhere, she'd have just WhatsApped me or told you in the bus. You live in the same building.'

But there was no going back. Not now. Ultimatum or no ultimatum.

'You nuts? Who'll leave a phone trail? And a letter seems romantic, right?' Pushy looked at me for support. I shook my head.

'Let's go. How much timepass are we going to do?'

I gave Pushy a shove and we left.

~

It was still raining. Downstairs, the ground was a sea of umbrellas. Would that have put the Mahadik gang off, I wondered as I got my umbrella and went down. The clouds had darkened everything. The boys on their way to the canteen across the road were crowding the footpath. They came there not to chat but to make passes at girls. They were down in the mud. So were we. Not even four steps further and I was already cursing the rain and the muck underfoot. The pattern of splatter began to form on the back of my legs, beneath my uniform shorts.

Saumya's durbar was in full swing. She saw me and waved wildly, like one of those heroines in an old Hindi film, getting off a plane and waving to the hero who's come to receive her. She took her time, making it conspicuous, elaborate.

'Overacting,' I mumbled.

'What?' Pushy asked.

'Nothing.'

Saumya gave me a V for Victory sign and then asked, 'Where?' using her hand again. Or maybe she meant, 'Just you two? Where's Bhavin?'

I shrugged.

Then an umbrella shifted and Mahadik peered out. He must have seen Saumya's gesticulations.

As per plan.

Saumya signalled me to wait and began a series of gestures whose meaning even she would have found difficult to understand.

However, they served their purpose: of drawing attention to both of us. I knew this since other umbrellas began to be brushed aside and people began to look at us. We pretended to be unaware of this and continued to 'talk' to each other while Pushy kept an eye on the staircase to see if anyone was coming along with Saumya's letter.

'She sent Vedant with the letter. He's got his Mickey Mouse umbrella with him. He's nuts, this Vedant. Just because he's short, he thinks he's a kid or what? Is this the age for Mickey Mouse merchandise?' Pushy asked, zipping his *Twilight* windcheater up to his neck. I had my back to the staircase but I wasn't going to change my place now.

'Let him come. Tell me when he gets close.'

'Two-three minutes, I think. Okay, he's at the security desk. Now he's talking to Reema from his class. He's pointing at us. Okay, he's reached Mahadik. The letter's in his hand. Hold on, Sant's noticed it. He's telling

Mahadik something.' Now his voice changed. 'Rohan. Problem! He's stopped him.'

'Who?'

'Mahadik. Who else? There's some trouble going on.'

'What brought him there? He should have come from the other direction and straight to us,' I was annoyed.

'Doesn't matter. We have to interfere,' Pushy began to panic. 'We don't have a choice, Rohan. Mahadik's got him by the neck. Quick,' Pushy ran off without stopping to check whether I was with him or not.

For a moment, I couldn't think. I hadn't calculated on something like this happening. If anything went down today, Dad wouldn't give me time for explanations before he packed my bags for boarding school. When I turned, I saw that Pushy was right. The time for calculations was past. Vedant was about to get a beating.

'I think I have given you enough rope,' Dad's voice echoed in my head. I looked at Saumya. She and Shreya were looking at us, one hand on the parapet. I had to do something. Almost without knowing it, I lowered my umbrella. As the rain came down and blurred my vision, the world turned smudgy and unreal, as if seen through a wet windshield. Through the haze, I could see Vedant on the receiving end of a terrific slap. His umbrella was missing too.

The letter fell from his hand into the mud. Sant was about to pick it up when Pushy fell upon him and they landed in the muck too. Mahadik let go of Vedant to deal with Pushy. Jello had vanished, probably to call in a teacher or a supervisor. I had wanted to teach Mahadik a lesson and here was my chance. No need to lure him to the jatra. No elaborate planning needed. I had wanted chaos as cover and here was chaos in front of me. Be careful what you wish for!

I wanted to laugh but now there was no point controlling it. So I let rip. I turned my umbrella into a sword and threw myself into the fray.

~

That's all I remember clearly. It's not as if I remember nothing at all. I have flashes but it's like one of those montages you see in an English film, no continuity. And for some strange reason, I see myself in the third person. In sepia tones and in slow motion.

If this were an ordinary memory, it is a commonplace that I should not have been able to see myself.

I should only remember what I had seen. So perhaps this is a memory which I or my mind composed later, pulling in the versions I heard from Pushy and Saumya and Mayuresh Sir, who had been summoned on to the scene by Jello, who ran as fast as his fat legs could take him.

One of those flashes is of me clubbing Mahadik on the head with my umbrella. A new umbrella, but an old-fashioned one. Bhavin and I had brought matching umbrellas only last month. Not the folding type. These were good, stout umbrellas with wooden handles. The cloth is actually green but in the flashback, it has the colour of mud.

Mahadik pushes Vedant aside and raises his hands to block the blows.

I'm a little too quick for him. The umbrella gets him somewhere between the cheek and the ear and I hear a sound like something breaking; a tooth perhaps, if he's lucky.

Mahadik topples over.

~

The second flash is as if I'm rubbing my eyes real fast. My eyes are on fire and my hand hurts. Someone has thrown muck into my eyes. Sant, if Pushy is to be believed. I don't remember. I try to clear my vision with the rain pelting down now. There are crowds too, I feel, but no one I recognize.

~

Third and last flash: Sant bites my arm, his teeth clamping down hard. Blood flows. Pushy tries to pull him off, grabs his hair. My eyes are still gritty. When my attention is drawn downwards, I can see Mahadik fallen. I don't know if the rain had got really dense or if it was only my imagination but I cannot see more than three or four feet in front of me. Some sounds come through.

Including a scream.

Saumya's, I think.

~

I don't like the Prajapati Subramaniam International School much. As I expected, I had to change schools within the week. In all that went down, I sustained a hairline fracture. Mahadik spent a couple of days in hospital.

Lots of people saw that he started it by grabbing Vedant and lighting into him. So I was home free. Sant also got hurt a bit but he didn't say much against me. Perhaps that's why no action was taken against me; I was just bundled out of school and ended up here.

Don't get me wrong; it's a good school. The curriculum is the same; it's IB, like our world school and since it's a boarding school it must be at least two or three lakhs out of Dad's pocket even without tuition. And he was right. It's nothing like home. In a way, he must be relieved. He never knew what to make of me. Like the other unpredictable things in life that he likes to eliminate, this affair has removed me from his world. Things must be running smoothly in his world. Aai must be getting time now to see the Marathi serials with ads and no more bad influence for any of my friends.

So no complaints. So at one level, it seems to be working out for all of us. I am a bit lonely and I am awesomely bored but I am not bitter about it. Maybe it's all for the best. Trust me on this one, it's all for the best.

HOME

'REZA, SAM, SAY BYE TO AAJI,' MAKARAND SAID AND dragged the kids in front of the screen to say their farewells.

Who knows what they are thinking? Reza is fourteen years old now and next month Sameer will be eleven. It's an odd time, one in which children change drastically. Their friends begin to mean more to them than their families; the distance between generations increases. So I often wonder how they will take a change in their family at this stage. Sameer is okay. He's still young. When he comes to India, we get on like a house on fire. But as for Reza... Makarand was saying that he is a little worried about her too. He says she has a Japanese friend now. Never mind. Prabhakar used to say what isn't on your doorstep shouldn't worry you, but where is my doorstep?

'Okay, Aai,' Makarand was saying. Having liberated the children, he was back on the screen. 'You get ready. I'll sort out my work and come on holiday. I'll stay fifteen days at least. But when I return, you have to come with me. If anything is left, we can take care of it later. Chal bye. Don't worry.' Makarand vanished and the square screen of Skype was left hanging before my eyes. Then finally I inched the curser up across the screen to the X in the right-hand corner and closed it. Then I clicked on another shortcut and the green board of Solitaire opened and a row of cards began to clatter into place. I turned the cards by habit but my mind was not on it.

It's been about five years now since Prabhakar has gone. When he was alive both of us did go to Chicago, to Makarand but those were short visits, a maximum of a couple of months. Prabhakar couldn't stay away from home very long. We would always say that we were coming for four or five months and then in a month or so, Prabhakar would have had enough. Actually, there was no real reason for us to come back to India because whatever we were doing here we could as well be doing there. It wasn't as if Prabhakar had friends whom he could not live without. It wasn't as if he had to come back for work either. In order to be able to say no, he had signed up for a PhD on the influence of the *Natyashastra* on the modern stage or something like that. That was really something to fill time. After having taught Marathi at the MA level for twenty-five years, he had wanted some way to stay connected to the university and had found this one. This meant that he could go and sit in the library and chat about literary matters with his friends. Otherwise it was all about a lot of reading and very little writing. Whether he had done this here or there would not really have mattered but it was not in his nature to just lie about. After about a month or so, Prabhakar would begin to remember various commitments. Nothing big. For instance, he would have to pick up some of his books from the senior lecturer who had been appointed in his place or he had promised to give some lecture to the third-year BA students or there was a conference on aesthetics that he would like to attend...one or two reasons like that. As he piled them up, Makarand would eventually throw up his hands and go out and buy us two tickets home. What lovely tickets they were. They looked like cheque books; only their pages were thin and shiny. When you looked at them, it felt as if you were about to embark on something important. These days the e-ticket printed out on ordinary paper seems like nothing. Everything has changed now.

I refreshed the Solitaire game which was stubbornly refusing to resolve itself. I called Banjo and went to get myself a glass of water and to refresh his water dish. The huge Samsung 300-litre fridge had a matka next to it and I took some water from it and turned to fill Banjo's bowl when it seemed as if someone had kicked me in the knees.

Banjo's red feeding plate and blue-green bowl were no longer there.

How could they be?

After Banjo went, I myself had...

I pulled up a chair from those near the dining table and sat down with a thump. It had been ten days since Banjo's death. I had cried many tears but it was still raw.

In his own way, Prabhakar had also been very fond of

Banjo. He called him a wild cat but he also kept a careful eye on his diet. If he didn't seem well Prabhakar would take him to the vet. And after Prabhakar, who was left to me but Banjo?

Makarand, of course. But he has his own life in America. From time to time he'd find an excuse to come to India. He'd check whether I needed any money and bring his children for the mandatory culture-shock trip. What else could he do? For many years, he had been insisting that we come to Chicago. But what am I supposed to do there? I don't like reading too much and unlike some of the women in our society, I don't care that much for religious observances. Which means I'd spend the whole day watching TV or sleeping. On top of that, Nandini also has a job. She has been working with the Red Cross for many years and I'd be another burden on her. All this while, Banjo had been one reason for me not to go. He'd become an excuse for both me and Makarand. But now even he…

No tears. Easy to say, but hard to do. I splashed my face with water and went into our bedroom. In the last four or five days the entire room had changed its appearance.

I had changed it myself. I had to start somewhere and apart from a few books in the hall, most of our personal belongings were in the bedroom. I had to make up my mind; what I would take, what I would put into long-term storage and what I would throw away.

I had to sort out the financial papers. I thought I

would spend the day looking at all the files and take out the papers that were not needed.

As I opened the bedroom door, my gaze fell on the photograph of Prabhakar and me, taken at the India Gate. Reza was young enough to be on Prabhakar's shoulders. The year was 2000, when Prabhakar had won the Best Teacher Award, presented by the President. That was when the photograph had been taken, on Makarand's new Nikon, a digital camera. What a lovely week we had in Delhi. Makarand and Nandini had come to India just for this, bringing little Reza with them.

All of us stayed at Hotel Samrat and wandered around the city to our hearts' content. We met some of Prabhakar's college friends who were now in New Delhi. It was to commemorate those days that we had enlarged the photograph and set it in a nice two-by-two-and-a-half-foot frame. Makarand was of the opinion that we should put the award certificate with its official signature along with this picture into a fine double mount, but Prabhakar would have none of it. He said that if there was some value to it then it was the memories of that day, and the photo represented that much better than any stupid certificate. Once he got an idea in his head there was no shifting him.

When we returned from Delhi, the certificate vanished and I never saw it again until he was gone and I was clearing out his cupboard. It was carefully hidden under a pile of rarely used blazers, folded with his trademark neatness.

What will become of this photograph? Taking the huge frame on to an aeroplane would be difficult. And thinking practically, why bother? It was not a rare photograph nor was it old. Makarand had taken the picture so he would have the image file with him. He could have it framed for me if I wanted. I knew what he would say: when you have so much else to take, why bother with things you can get there? He would be right too. But it was also true that a new print would be identical but it would never be the same.

I picked up a piece of mulmul and gently wiped the dust off the glass. Not much dust. After all, I clean it every day. But when you're shifting all the old files and albums to clear them out, you expect some dust. Looking at that photo, I thought of the Reza of that time. How cute she looked, how chubby! And always smiling. She's tall now and the smile is missing. Maybe it turns up when she's with her friends but it seems an effort for her to smile when I am around. It's as if some other unrecognizable girl has been substituted. Now I'm supposed to go and live there. How will she react?

And Samir? Even though he insists so much, I can't bring myself to call him Sam and he's a bit put off by that too.

Up to now any contact with these children had been limited to a couple of weeks each year. And some of that would be spent in Bengaluru with Nandini's parents. So even if the blood tie is direct, our relationship is slight. How would this change? Makarand says they'll get used to me. I'll become a habit. A habit? Do I want to be a habit?

The mobile rang and brought me to my senses. I looked around but could not see it anywhere. I must have left it in the study, next to the computer. Whether a phone is fixed or cordless or a mobile, there is no way to free oneself from its imperious summons. The changes in technology make no difference. You still have to run after it. Leaving it in odd places and forgetting it is an old habit with me. Maybe it's hereditary. I can remember clearly that my father too was in the habit of mislaying things. He died so young, not even forty-five. He would lose typical things: files, papers, bags. Aai would call him 'The Absent-minded Professor' after the Disney film. I don't think there is a cure.

Not only was the phone not near the computer, it was not even in that room. I looked under some papers but it wasn't there. I glanced at the bookshelf. No, the sound was coming from without. Maybe from the kitchen? By the time I got to the kitchen—and my speed isn't what it used to be—the ringing stopped. I was a bit relieved. These days, I don't get many important calls: there's Charu, my friend from the Elphinstone College; Makarand of course; and Prabhakar's nephew who lives in Hindu Colony. The rest are all cold callers or salesmen.

The phone was right there on the shelf by the microwave. I couldn't recognize the number but it was the kind where a pair of digits repeats itself. Not a residential number. Either someone asking for a donation or someone with the details of a 'scheme'. Relieved, I filled a tumbler with water and drank it off.

I went back to the bedroom with as much waste paper as I could carry. I dropped it on the bed and took out the Scotch tape from a drawer from the side table. One should not use Scotch tape for packing, Prabhakar used to say. It doesn't stick and it gets loose. But I didn't have an option. I wasn't going to lay my hands on any other kind of tape and as long as that Delhi photo hung there, I didn't think I could do anything substantial.

I went inside and tried to lift the bottom of the frame to dislodge it but it wouldn't budge. It was heavy but that wasn't it. It had got stuck somewhere. The last time Makarand had been in town, there had been no question of me leaving my home but now… When he arrives, he can easily take it down for me. But nothing will happen until the frame is off the wall. I've decided the frame goes. So it must go.

~

It's been many months since I opened the little door by the side of the kitchen and set foot in the dry balcony. What need to come here? As it is, there's more space than I need in the house now. Prabhakar said that he had bought a flat in this building of huge flats so that Makarand would have a room of his own. But I suspect the large house was his dream. Because he settled down here before Makarand or I did. It took Makarand a while to make friends, but he did. Not me. What if our Thane flat had one bedroom and was half the size of this one? I still liked it better. When Prabhakar got his first job, he'd registered for it. When we married, he got possession so it really felt like home to me in every way. It had small rooms, it was easy to tidy, and though it was stuffed with things, it was manageable. The grocer was across the road. We knew our neighbours. It was a seven-minute walk from Makarand's school. This society has so many rich families that the atmosphere is a little more formal than I like. I have been here so many years but I have been unable to make friends with a single person. Okay, I did get to know one family: Sanika and Sushrut in 5B but that's a names-only thing. And only because that boisterous dog Robie kept harassing Banjo.

Of late, I had decided not to use the dry balcony. The clothes dry in the machine anyway. And if it comes to that, I line up all the chairs from the dining table, spread the clothes on them, turn on the fan and let them dry. The dry balcony is where the unused stuff is kept. After hunting a little, I found what I was looking for: a small wooden stepladder. I had insisted on bringing it from Thane. It was tucked between Makarand's old cycle and Prabhakar's easel.

It isn't a very tall ladder but it serves to get one up to the height needed for shelves and lofts. In Thane, the house was filled with cupboards and they were all stuffed. When we left, Prabhakar made it clear that we weren't taking all that we had with us just because we had it. Each thing, each object was subjected to a rigorous examination. If such-and-such object were not with us, could we manage? If so-and-so thing had not been touched in a year, what were the chances that we would need it again? Then we should 'ruthlessly' (his word) get rid of what we did not need, thus freeing ourselves…and so before we came here, we had liberated ourselves of half of our belongings and the rest looked lost and forlorn in this huge new space. Nothing had to be hoisted up on to the upper shelves and so the ladder had remained unused. It became unnecessary too. Touching it now raised goosebumps on my skin. How many years since I had touched it? What should I have felt if someone had told me then that next time I touched the ladder, both Prabhakar and Banjo would be gone? For a moment, I leaned against the wall and counted my breaths.

Someone had told me that when I get excited, I should count my breaths to calm myself. I closed my eyes and concentrated on my breath. Inhale-exhale, inhale-exhale…I opened my eyes when there was some improvement.

I took a duster from the stand and gave the ladder a good wipe down. Then I opened the door and fixed it on the magnetic doorstop and picked up the ladder with both hands and began to carry it to the bedroom. I began to feel better.

The ladder had its own support so it did not have to be leaned against the wall. In these matters I am rather fastidious. Those lean-to ladders spoil the paint on the walls…and then you can't repaint one area, you have to do the whole room again.

Which is why I have this special ladder that does not need to be leaned against a wall. I picked my way through all the things I had brought into the bedroom and set the ladder down near the frame. Some papers here and there, some folded were flapping around. I stepped around them and unhooked the ladder and set it up neatly. I placed a hand carefully on the wall and climbed on to the first rung. Then the next. The ladder creaked a little but it held. Poor thing, it had been lying in a corner for so long. Now that I had brought it in, I ought to have given it a thorough once-over. If given an oiling, it will serve for years yet. But who will it serve? We have to shift. You don't know what you will need and when. I have been thinking about leaving this house since morning. I even spoke to Makarand on Skype. What will affect a person suddenly, deeply, is anyone's guess. Then I started the process of clearing up. My mind was calm, but this ladder…

I do not care for such emotions. For a moment, I closed my eyes tightly before climbing the next step. Now I could reach the top of the frame easily, but there was a problem. I was now quite close to the top of the ladder but there was no one around to hold it steady. The question was not what would happen now but what would happen when the weight of the frame and my weight had to be borne by the ladder. Would it hold? But what option did I have? Who else was in the house? I could call the security guard and tip him fifty rupees. He seems like a trustworthy person. But the stories one reads in the newspapers these days! And I live alone. Why put temptation in anyone's way?

Finally, I decided to be brave. I placed one foot and then the next on the final rung and made myself as secure as possible. I wiped my hands on my pallu and then took firm hold of the frame and tried to lift it up. As I suspected, something was indeed stuck. I began to work it loose. It began to give and so I got brave and tried a yank. And then…

~

When I came to my senses, for a couple of minutes I had no idea where I was. I wondered: why am I lying on the floor? My left ear felt cold. I picked myself up and leaned against the wall.

I couldn't see very clearly and the pressure cooker was whistling. I thought: time to turn the gas low, it's whistled, and then everything began to come back. Where do we use the cooker now? I don't even cook these days. So what was I doing?

The frame! The ladder!

The ringing stopped and the room came into focus all at once. Then I saw splinters of glass, the glass from the frame broken…and blood. The ladder was on its side, resting on a pile of files and a Marathi book was open wide, its pages spattered with blood.

Timidly, I moved my hand; but I did not feel the pain I expected. I gathered myself and tried to stand. This would not be possible, I reasoned, if I had broken a bone or something. But things weren't so bad: I did manage to get up. However, I didn't want to be too courageous. So I leaned against the wall and stayed that way.

From this position, however, things looked worse, almost frightening. Glass, ladder, the pile of books overturned by the ladder, the blood all over them, the bottle of water overturned too, the water diluting the blood and spreading it further. I grabbed a bedsheet and threw it over the water to stop its progress. And without bothering to check whether this had worked or not, I walked to the dressing table. I wanted to look at myself in the mirror and check the extent of the damages.

Earlier, the sight of blood would make me dizzy. It was so severe a reaction that if there was no one to support me, I'd land on the floor. When I had to visit someone in the hospital, I would try to postpone it, and when I did have to go I would grab Prabhakar's hand as we entered the hospital and I would cling to it, as to a lifeline, until we left. But today, no giddiness. So was that psychosomatic? Had I allowed myself the luxury of giddiness as long as I knew there would be someone to get hold of me before I fell? But now that there was nobody around…

The image in the mirror was rather disturbing. The blood on my forehead had dried. My hair was sticky with clotted blood. I don't know how but I hadn't even considered the state of my sari up to this point of time but now, I saw a big dark stain on it. The glass had ripped it too. There was blood on my hands. There was no way to know just where I was hurt and how much. I lacked the courage to find out.

My head began to throb. Darkness began to cloud my eyes. I had to do something and quickly. The phone began to ring but I didn't have the strength to look for it.

The only name that came to mind was Sushrut; why, I could not imagine. One simple explanation could be that this is the only household I have any connection with, good or bad. They were nice people. I had heard rumours that they were not married; but what does it matter to me? Look at the times we live in. Soon the gossip will be about a young couple who choose to marry instead of just living together. Also he might be at home right now. I vaguely remember him saying something about being between jobs. But was that the only reason? Makarand had given me the number for one of his friends, a doctor, to call in an emergency. His nursing home is quite close to the colony too. I just didn't seem to have the energy to find the number and call him. I waited until I felt a bit better and got up, determined to find Sushrut. I can't imagine now how I reached his home.

When Sushrut opened the door, a cloud of cigarette smoke enveloped me—and the sound of his dog barking. The memory of Banjo came back, a slash of pain.

For a moment, Sushrut was transfixed. It was as if he were playing that game 'Statue', where children freeze when someone shouts 'Statue'. It must have been the sight of me. But then he was galvanized into action. When I lost consciousness again, I was thinking of the smell of cigarettes. How come I'd never noticed that he smoked before this?

~

When I woke again, it was because of the smell of medicine in the room. I opened my eyes to see Sushrut sitting on the visitor's bed. In his hands was a copy of *The Catcher in the Rye* but he wasn't looking at it. The hospital bed was against a wall in which a window was set. Through this you could see a patch of sky. Evening was coming on. Sushrut was staring out of the window. As I looked at him, it became clear that he was not looking at anything specific. He was looking into the void.

'I didn't know you smoked.' The sound of my voice startled Sushrut and his gaze turned to me.

He smiled seeing me awake. 'No, Joshi Kaku. I don't smoke.' He was silent. Then he said: 'That was my first cigarette. No, maybe my second. I did try one in school.'

I said nothing.

'Kaku, we can go home if you want,' he said, setting the book aside. 'They say you're okay now. You were out for the count so the doctor said we had to wait until you woke up. I called Makarand to keep him updated. He'd given me his Chicago number the last time he was here. I told him you'll call when you get back home. He said he'd wait for your call.'

In the car Sushrut chattered on a fair bit. I told him what had happened. He said he'd come and help me the next morning with the frame and the packing, on the condition that tonight I do not even go into that room.

After a while, he said quietly, 'I have to start packing too. For both of us.'

I didn't know if it was appropriate to say anything.

He continued: 'Sanika is off to the US at the end of the month. For six months. Company work.'

'And you?' I asked the obvious.

'Me? Not fixed yet. You know we're not exactly…I mean…' he fumbled.

'Yes. I heard. What difference does it make? You are together, no?'

'I guess.'

'What's to guess? You have doubts?'

'No, not that way.'

'No, just that way.'

'I have this dream of being a popular writer,' he said, not taking his eyes from the road. 'Even in college, I used to write. But when I started out on my career, I could never find the time. Now Sanika has this grand idea that I go with her to Seattle and use the time to write.'

'Wonderful. What's the problem?'

'No problem really. It's just that I had some ideas about how a home should be and this upsets them all. Don't get me wrong. I'm not a traditional male chauvinist who thinks the man should be the provider and the woman should be the homemaker and that these rules are fixed. But this is the complete reversal of that and all so sudden. I can't figure it out. And now there's no time to think. I have said I'll go but I'm not convinced.'

The silence was broken only by the sound of a gear change.

The society gates up ahead. Darkness falling.

'I was confused. I am confused. So I was smoking. Someone said smoking reduces your tension and helps you make a decision.'

I managed not to laugh but Sushrut must have guessed. He was embarrassed.

'Sorry, I'm off-loading this ridiculous problem on you. As if you haven't enough of your own.'

He parked the car in the basement and we got down. Perhaps it was the effect of the painkillers, but I was not in pain. If only there were an anaesthetic that would numb him to social conventions, I would have given Sushrut a good strong dose.

'What does a home mean, Sushrut?' I asked the question that was circling in my head.

'Hmm?' he was surprised.

'You said you had some ideas about what a home should be so I brought it up. What does a home mean? The space in which you live? Or the people and the web of relationships they spin? Or the roles they live out and those they assign each other? Does that make a home?'

Sushrut said nothing right up to my floor. I didn't push him to speak either.

But it was clear he was thinking.

Perhaps he had called Sanika for, she was standing outside my door when we got there. After Banjo, what distance remained between us had been erased and we had begun to chat as pet-owners do.

Sanika made coffee and we sat over it for a long time,

both insisted that I was to call them if I needed anything. Sushrut said he would come in the morning to help and they left.

When I closed the master bedroom and went into the study to call Makarand, I saw the mobile right in front of me. There were four missed calls—all from the same number. I was about to set it aside when it rang again. The same number. Someone really wanted to talk to me. I answered and, 'Madam, our bank offers you home loan up to eighty lakhs rupees…'

I wanted to laugh. If these banks keep at it, soon there will be no housing problem at all. But I wasn't worried about the housing woes of the world. I had solved my own. Whether Sushrut ever answered the question I had posed to him, I would not know. But in asking it, I had found my own answer. For better or worse, my life would be in Chicago now, among my own. There was no reason to cling to these four walls in a congested city. What was left here for me? The memories?

They would come with me to Chicago. It would be foolish to remain stuck in the past. It would be equally foolish to ignore reality.

I had decided. This time when I called Makarand, there was a new energy inside me, something I hadn't felt for a while.

BHARDWAJ

I HAD A BOOK OF NURSERY RHYMES WHEN I WAS IN THE second or third standard. Someone must have given it to me, or it must have come down through the family. Because I can never remember it being new. It was a hardback with good, thick paper inside. Not the glossy art paper of fashion catalogues. This had a matt finish. Although my memory of it is a bit vague now, I seem to remember a fine texture too. The cover had been torn off at some time but on the dirty, white spine, you could see its name. In a dignified font. I don't remember the exact name now. 'Essential Nursery Rhymes' or something like that. Inside, lovely illustrations. Not cartoons, nothing patched together in a hurry. I have the feeling this book had something to do with my love of art. It was copying these illustrations that started me off on my self-education. Later, the lessons I learned from this book came in handy when I got admission in architecture.

Anyway, one of the poems was 'Who Killed Cock Robin?' Perhaps you know it. It may not be as popular as 'Jack and Jill' but it is fairly well-known. First, everyone is asked who killed Cock Robin and the sparrow says he did it. Then a fish catches his blood and the beetle says he'll stitch the shroud and the rook says he'll play priest and so on. Although it was a child's book, I remember the illustration: A photo-realistic depiction of a dead bird with an arrow sticking out of its chest and blood pouring from the wound.

I never forgot the picture. That day, while inspecting a slab on the fortieth floor of Elena's site, I saw a dead Bhardwaj—a crow pheasant, it's called—and remembered the illustration again. It was lying on a small pile of steel bars.

How had it died? Had one of the steel bars pierced it as it had in the poem? Seeing a Bhardwaj is supposed to be lucky but a dead one?

'Sir!'

Nita's voice startled me. I had forgotten she was with me. Nita is my personal assistant. I don't need a personal assistant really. I've told Sanika and Anant this a hundred times. If I need help, there's Partho who can sit in on meetings. But they just won't listen. Protocol is protocol, they say. They have a point but Nita is more pain than profit. My meetings aren't the kind Sanika and Anant have, over design or material selection, project reports and updates. My meetings tend to be confidential, one-on-one things. Nita can't stand in for me if I can't make it. This means I have to find her something else to do or let her loose on Partho. Since he does most of the follow-up, he often needs help.

'Sir?' she said again, 'Sanika Ma'am on the line.'

I took the phone.

'Sanika.'

'Agashe, what's wrong with your phone?'

I pulled it out of my pocket. Battery dead. Silly of me. I had forgotten the charger today—and iPhone chargers are hard to find. Luckily, I have one in the car.

'Problem with the battery. What's up?'

Sanika never calls just like that. She always has a reason. No different today.

Sanika must be one of the smartest persons I know. Anant and I met her when we were in the final year. At a ragging session. She had just been admitted to college. Truth to tell, we weren't really interested in ragging. But I had discovered early that it was best to mingle with the crowd. You can use its collective strength and you can even fit in a good deed or two. Anant didn't get this. To him, it was what it was. But he went along because of me.

That day our good deed was to extract Sanika from the clutches of a second-year jock. Perhaps it was just the excitement of becoming a senior or something more than that but he was insistent in his pursuit. Actually, Sanika was on top of it. The way things were going, even if we had not intervened, she would have macerated him and served him up on a piece of toast.

~

'Antya has been desperately trying to get in touch with you for the last hour. He even tried Partho's cell to see if you two are together. Apparently not, but anyway, he wants to meet you immediately. It's something to do with Elena and he wants to meet you in person.'

'I'm on the site. Don't worry. I'll call him,' I said and told Nita to call Anant.

~

It must have been at our first or second meeting that Sanika started calling Anant Antya. That gives you some sense of her self-confidence. To date, she is the only person who calls him that. Most juniors walk in fear of their seniors but Sanika was unconcerned. But she wasn't brash either. She was a straight-talking girl; she looked you in the eye and she got your number. It was this self-confidence that had convinced us to involve her when we thought of starting our own architecture firm. Up to then, her only real experience had been in NGO work. But that didn't show. She fitted in smoothly, effortlessly, with high-end clients, with the suits and the corporates. We never regretted asking her. Sanika has only one problem, then as now. She is too upright, professionally speaking. Perhaps it's because her father was in the armed forces or something but she is always going on about how we need to keep SNA on the straight and narrow. Personally, I have no objection but in the financial capital of India where the stakes are always so high, how can you guarantee that?

But we protect her as much as we can, as far as we can. And so far, so good.

'Sir, Anant Sir on the line.'

'Tell me.'

'Where are you now?' Anant seemed worried.

'Elena. Why?'

'How long will it take you to get to the Churchgate Coffee Day?'

'Fifteen minutes?'

'Make it twenty-five. I'm crossing Byculla.'

'See you there,' I said and hung up.

As soon as I heard his voice, I could tell what the problem was and what the possible solution could be. Anant is given to these irrational panic attacks. We've often dealt with roadblocks. The good thing about being in a fast-paced city like Mumbai is that it works to everyone's benefit to keep things going. So if there's a roadblock, someone else will know how to clear it away. There are always going to be ways and means. Not 100 per cent foolproof. Not guaranteed. But they're there. And the ends justify the means.

No point taking Nita with me so I sent her off with Panse to a meeting that is supposed to shortlist composite panels for the wall cladding for the Chatterjee Group's Bandra-Kurla Complex project and told her to go straight back to the office afterwards. I started the car, put the phone to charge. The hands-free was connected and so I began to call even as I turned the car out of the lot.

Problems are meant to be solved. There are only three important questions. How soon can you get to the root of the problem? How important is it for you to deal with it? How far will you go to solve it?

I said fifteen minutes but it wasn't easy. I start work early. So even after visiting the Elena site, it was only 11:15. Morning traffic was heavy. It wasn't wasting my time; I was on the phone.

I've found that once you know what needs to be done, it doesn't take you long to do it. But I kept an eye on my watch anyway and pushed the car through and made it to the Churchgate signal in twenty-two minutes.

Driving in Mumbai is painful; I find it a bore but I couldn't manage without a car. I have so many meetings to get through every day that even having a car at my disposal isn't the ideal solution. Sanika doesn't use her car but her solution—train travel—seems cosmetic at best. Because once she gets to the office by train, there's always someone's car she can use if she has to go somewhere.

~

I turned into the next lane after Churchgate and shoved the keys and a hundred-rupee note into the hands of the first Pay-and-Park attendant I could see. Now parking wasn't my headache. I picked up my iPad and was out. Many of the staff find it odd that I do not use a laptop. Actually, there's nothing odd about it. Why would I need a laptop? I don't use Autocad myself. I have staff for that. Why keep a dog and bark?

Everyone has his or her job which only he or she can do. I don't see my job as sitting at a drawing board. I'm an overseer. I get things done.

Half an hour after I left Elena, I entered CCD. It's

generally empty at this time and so it was now. Outside, a boy in his early twenties was sketching on tracing paper. A cigarette dangled from his mouth.

I couldn't see what he was drawing but he seemed to have a near-professional hand. When I came in, he saw me and looked away. Then recognition flared and he looked up again. He quickly put out the cigarette and stuck it back in the packet. The packet seemed filled with stubs.

His face seemed familiar. One of the young ones who come in for training? Perhaps. But I don't really deal with them and I don't clutter my mind with the unimportant. Even if he seemed to find me familiar, it could be that he was an architecture student. The three of us had appeared on the cover of *Indian Architect & Builder* when the magazine did a story on the firm.

We were photographed in our conference room, with Sanika sitting in a chair of her own design and both of us standing on either side of her. The accompanying story mentioned all our big projects in the past five years but the emphasis was on the design process that had led to Elena. People sometimes recognize us because of that cover. Generally, people in the profession or allied fields. Otherwise what star value do architects have? Would most people recognize Hafeez Contractor?

I pushed past the swing doors. Inside all the tables were empty except for a couple in a corner, about the same age as the young man outside. They seemed to be casual friends; no unseemly public display of affection.

There weren't many people in the coffee shop. It wasn't cold either. Perhaps they'd only just started up the air conditioning. I took off my blazer and draped it over the chair in front of me. I ordered a mineral water at the counter and sat down. The sketching boy was visible from where I was sitting. Another young fellow had joined him, but he didn't look familiar. I began to feel like I was spying on the two so I checked my Powermail and then began to browse the Arts section of *The New York Times* app.

I had read two articles by the time Anant arrived: One was a review of an installation by a feminist artist; the other, a profile of an Asian sculptor. It was a much-hyped name; I'd heard about him but didn't know anything about his work. It seemed interesting but also a little frivolous. I made a mental note to check on some of his other work and shut my iPad when Anant arrived. I ordered cappuccinos for both of us and said, 'Tell me.'

Actually, he didn't seem to be in any shape to say much. I know his panic mode well but this was a little worse than usual. Generally, he can spend an entire day going to meetings and kissing up to clients and still look bandbox fresh, but he was looking a little worse for the wear and it wasn't even afternoon. He had bags under his eyes, his hair was tousled, his shirt crumpled.

'Did you run all the way from Byculla?' I asked partly out of worry and partly to lighten his mood. He pretended not to hear.

'Didn't I warn you not to take on Elena?' He went straight to the point.

'Relax, Anant. Don't get hyper. We had discussed the risks before we started. How many skyscrapers are coming up in Colaba, do you know? This was a chance to be part of history.'

'History!' Anant laughed loudly. So loudly that the couple behind us began to look in our direction. Mechanically almost, I checked the sketching boy. Of the two, only one was left. The one who had come later. But he wasn't looking at us. Anant's laugh hadn't got that far; or the boy was deep in his own thoughts.

'Relax. What's got you so upset?'

'What's happened has got me upset,' he said and picked up the bottle of water and drank it in thirsty gulps. 'I don't have the details. But there's been a mess up. I just got a call from the ministry. They want a meeting with you. There's going to be a stay put on Elena and the whole project will go under the scanner.'

'Scanner? Why?'

'Who knows? They'll find something. Isn't there enough? The FSI increase for one. The plot being reserved for a school for another. Anything. All of the above.'

His face was grey with worry. I kept drinking my coffee peacefully. He expected me to get upset. My peaceful attitude got him even more rattled.

'What are you really worried about?' I asked, setting my mug aside and wondering if I should order another.

I don't drink, not even cocktails, but coffee is an old habit. From college, I think. At first, it was to stay up to get submissions done. Then the coffee would keep me up nights and I'd drink more coffee just because I was up…a vicious circle. But almost everything ends up that way; vicious circles don't stop because they've outlived their usefulness. They become part of your life. It's as if this is the natural order of things. I drank the last gulp of mineral water and signalled to the kid at the counter for another cup.

Before I started on my second cappuccino, Anant had gone into brooding mode. This is his specialty. If you look at him, he doesn't look like someone who'll crumble in an emergency. He's crafted a perfect image for himself but it really is a mask. Not a mask for others but for himself. His formal clothes, his expensive pens, the superficial air of calm, all this makes up the mask. Once he slips it on, he can convince himself that he is up to whatever life throws at him. And so armed, he can go out and make deals with clients, harry the office staff and make the rules at home. That keeps him calm. But if things begin to get out of hand, his centre cannot hold.

This mask doesn't work with Sanika or me. We know him too well. Though we've never talked about it, we recognize these two avatars: there's Smart Anant and there's Scared Anant. Sanika once referred to him as Antya in a meeting, not really the best way to talk about a partner in an up-and-coming architectural practice like ours, but he didn't mind. Perhaps that is also suggestive.

'Calm down, Anant,' I said, but there was no sign of that happening. I never know how much I should tell him. Because the more he knows, the more he fears. But now it was necessary to take him into confidence. He wouldn't go back to normal otherwise.

'You remember Anant, what happened last week at the meeting with Rednecks?'

Now Anant was confused. He couldn't see the link between Elena and Rednecks. Rednecks Hospitality is a big client of ours. Basically, an American hotel chain. Head office in Seattle. They have properties under development at a couple of places in Europe and India. We'd just got their Delhi five-star hotel done. They liked our work and suggested we bid for a multi-project proposal in the US. We got it. The projects get underway next month. When I mentioned Rednecks, I knew Anant would be surprised. After all, what could Elena, a sixty-storey tower which would house the rich and the famous in five-bedroom apartments in the country's most expensive area, and the Rednecks project have in common?

'What happened at the meeting?' Anant asked, his voice confused.

'You were to go to Seattle for six months, remember?' I asked, pushing backwards.

'Yes. And at the meeting you said I'd been worried about Rohan. So Sanika should go in my place.' Anant was trying to find the pattern but he could not see the dots. And then suddenly he got it. His expression changed. His tone became accusatory: 'You knew this was going to erupt. And that Sanika would have none of it. So you wanted her out of the way.'

I took another sip of coffee and continued to look at him.

'I thought you were acting out of concern about what happened at Rohan's school…' his voice trailed off as he looked at me, as if I had committed a crime. By the way, Rohan is Anant's son. Smart kid. A bit irrational. But who isn't at that age? Anant is worried sick about him. For no reason at all. I'm sure he'll grow out of it, but only if Anant gives him some space.

'Of course, I am concerned about Rohan,' I ignored his anger. 'But I don't see why you have to get after him all the time. Whatever his problems are, as he grows up, they'll go away. But this time I didn't act out of concern for him. It was only important that Sanika should think so. If she hadn't thought you were having family troubles, she would never have agreed to go. It was important to keep her away from the office for a while. I knew the Elena project was going to give us some headaches. Minor ones but headaches, nonetheless. It will be better for everyone if Sanika is not around.'

Now Anant looked as if someone had cheated him. As if I had cheated him really. No reason for that actually. I wasn't cheating Sanika or him. Just protecting them from the scandal that was going to break.

'To tell the truth, Anant, how would I imagine that this would get so big? But in the past month, wheels have been turning. However powerful your position is, it's difficult to keep everything under wraps at all times. I am told someone filed a complaint under the

Right to Information Act and got the Elena papers out and found some irregularities. Now that things are out, even the BMC won't be able to sit on it. Some nominal investigations will have to be made. I knew this was coming so I wanted Sanika out of the way. And as I keep telling you, I know what's going on. I'm in the loop. Even today, they only called you because my phone was out of reach. And they must have panicked. Don't worry, I'll handle it. We are registered as Elena's architects. So that will get to the papers. But the way I see it, no publicity is bad publicity. People who haven't heard about us before, will now. The public likes a scandal. And the bigger the scandal, the greater the glamour, the more the public likes it. Only nothing must be proved. And don't worry, nothing is going to be proved here.'

'How can you be sure?' Anant asked, but he was getting back to normal. The mask, which had slipped, was slowly moving back into place. The anger was abating but the sarcasm was now showing up. He was now fairly sure there was no danger to us and equally sure I would get us through and out, but he still felt he had been tricked. 'How can it not come back to us? Didn't you just say we are registered as the architects in the paperwork and proposals?'

'You have to trust me on this one, Anant. I said I'd handle it, right? I will. They need a scapegoat. I'm working on finding one,' I said, though I had the answers worked out. 'Who's the owner on this? Me, right? So don't get involved. I'll do the talking. It'll take about a month for it to lose steam. And our name will be mentioned but that's all that will happen.'

~

By the time I had talked him into a place where he felt secure, another twenty minutes had passed. It was noon now, the sun was right overhead. It was the monsoon but the sky was free of clouds. Generally, people like the early hours of the day. They like the dawn with its promise of a new day; or the dusk for romantic reasons. I like afternoons. Other times of day are better in comparison but they pass and their pleasantness passes too. Afternoons are not like that. Once you get used to afternoons, no other watch of the day can upset you. So you're always comfortable. Sometimes I feel that there must be another reason, something deeper than this. Something to do with memory; from the time when I was just starting out. After all, nostalgia is a powerful drug.

I suspect it has something to do with the time when I was a junior architect with Seth Consultants, Lamington Road. Every afternoon, I would catch a bus to go off for approvals. The planning department was then in the head office of the Corporation. You had to spend hours there. Sometimes you had to persuade people to help and sometimes you used other ways. But then I began to make friends with them. And the work got easier. Sometimes it would only take fifteen minutes before I was out of there again.

The books on the street, the pirated DVDs that had then just begun to show up, exhibitions at Jehangir or Chemould, vada pao on the steps of the Asiatic Library or the sugarcane juice at Fountain, all these came together to form my idea of a perfect afternoon. Those afternoons didn't just give me happiness, they also gave me the people skills I needed when we started our own practice. Anant and Sanika have other skills: design sense, client management, the kind of commanding presence an architect needs. But what I got out of those afternoons is mine alone.

I called the office and asked them to cancel all my appointments and began to walk. I needed time to think. I'd have to pay the parking attendant more but that didn't matter. What gets done without money here?

That day I did all the things I used to do and added some new ones. I switched off my phone and wandered lonely as a cloud. I looked at the books on the street. I went to the Asiatic Library and walked around Horniman Circle. I passed some time at the Study Corner in the garden there. Some young people were really studying. I allowed myself a little envy of their easy lives. I went to Rhythm House and bought Blu-ray discs of third-class new Hindi films just to fill up the mahogany display case I have at home. Who has the time to see the damned things now? I went to the Jehangir and saw a monsoon art show. At Samovar, I had more coffee and a sandwich. And then I let my feet lead me and street opened into street. I don't remember all the places I went but the

Gateway, the Taj Vivanta, the streets at Nariman Point and the new promenade that was already being dug up, the GPO and other such. I didn't think much about work. The more I walked, the more lost I felt. The area which I thought of as familiar territory seemed strange now. Everywhere new constructions had sprung up. You couldn't walk on the footpaths for the crowds and the roads were raging with noise. Everything was changing, getting uglier. Who was responsible for this change? I had once felt part of this area; now no longer. Or was it that the area looked on me as a stranger? Had my gaze changed? Or had its gaze changed? And when had this happened?

My confusion increased steadily and I kept walking. When I came to my senses, I was at a familiar spot. Elena's skeleton reared up in front of me. It was past five. The afternoon heat was receding. My favourite time of day was ending. I turned on my phone and a line-up of messages greeted me. I ignored them and slipped the phone into my pocket.

The junior engineer all but ran up to me when I went in. I stopped him in his tracks with a gesture and told him to get the lift operator. The temporary lift rose, shuddering, revealing Mumbai to me: a city intent on forgetting its past, on re-inventing itself.

I told the lift operator to stay where he was and went on alone. The Bhardwaj was still lying on the pile of iron rods. After I had left, no one had come this way. Once again, 'Who Killed Cock Robin?' began to play in my head. On one side, the sea. On the other, the city. A city that seemed to believe that the Queen's Necklace was enough past for it, a city sacrificing its beauty at the dirty altars of money. I thought, someone ought to write a poem on who killed the city of Mumbai.

Politicians who were bulldozing slums and selling off mill land; builders who were throwing up huge identical buildings everywhere, thus erasing all difference; architects like us who ignored the big picture and focused on their own self-interest; bureaucrats who had lost control over the number of people and cars and pointed mutely at development as they watched this slow death; and the ordinary citizen, unaware of the impending disaster.

And as the heat faded and as the image faded, I suddenly thought of the sketching boy at CCD, the one surprised to see me, the one who'd recognized me. In his eyes, I must have seemed a role model: already partner at a young and aggressive firm while still in my forties, with lots of money, great projects and so on. Thinking of his young and idealistic face, I wanted to exchange places with him.

My phone rang. Sanika.

'Agashe, what do you think has happened?' Sanika asked cheerfully.

'Happened? Something new?' I tried to keep my voice upbeat but she must have heard some different note.

'Your voice is odd. Is this a bad time? Are you with someone?'

'Nothing. Tell me. Go on,' I managed to get my voice back to normal.

'Arre, the Gujarat Urban Development Department called. They're putting together master plans for some of their major cities. They said we came highly recommended by our Municipal Corporation.'

That got me laughing. Master planning. They had come to the right place. There's no turning back now. I came back to myself, the depressing thoughts that had plagued me earlier dropped away. I was surprised at myself. Depressed? At this height? Why? Elena was only a beginning. The only important thing was to climb higher. So high that you could not see what had been left behind; or if you saw it, by some mistake, it should be unrecognizable.

I said I'd get to the office and take everyone out for a celebration. Anant and Sanika would wait for me. I had to get going quickly. There was no time to hang around here, no reason to.

I called the lift operator, showed him the dead bird and told him to get the area cleared. As I descended, the lights were going on in the city.

My mood had changed dramatically. You can say a dead Bhardwaj is also lucky.

COMPETITION

THE CLASS AT THE PANDARINATH THORAT GURUJI SCHOOL was not very big but in comparison to the tiny rooms at our school, it seemed huge, as if it could seat sixty students comfortably. A low platform in the middle with the chair and table and other teacher stuff on it. Behind, a blackboard with something written on it in coloured chalk. Probably the previous day's lesson. The walls were painted in the school's colours: dirty oil paint up to about three to three-and-a-half feet, of a quality that children could not damage and above that, a powdery white colour.

I entered the room, clinging to the wall because my navy blue pinafore had a white spot on its upper half that I had spent the day hiding. I didn't really like these elocution competitions. I had never put my name in for this one. But Pandarpattebai put me down without so much as asking me. I had a cousin, Nandita, who had a kind of record of winning these competitions. Nandita was a few years older than me and had finished her tenth standard. However last minute her entry, however unprepared, whatever the topic, she would go up on stage and deliver herself of a speech. Everyone thought she would go on the stage or into films but she went into Income Tax. I suppose Pandarpattebai thought I would carry on this tradition and so she thrust me on to the stage. She would not spare me, even in group songs and competitions. I had no interest in these things, but what was that to her? There's a time for everything. That day I think, my time had come.

There weren't many students in the class. I hadn't thought there'd be many. This was only a qualifying round. There must have seventeen or eighteen of us. One or two were teachers, the other girls and boys who were *sitting together*. That itself was a thrill since our school, Ramabai Karve, was an all-girls school. And so we knew that since this was an interschool competition, boys and girls would sit together. You could say that this was one of the chief attractions of the competition. This was an extempore elocution. There was a cane basket on the first bench. When your name was called, you drew a topic out of that basket. You got five minutes to think about it and then you had to go up and speak for five to seven minutes.

I could tell when it started that the children had prepared well. One or two fumbled for words, a couple stopped speaking halfway but most did well. How would I stand up to them? I had never participated in an elocution like this one. I did not even like public speaking. I had no interest in it either. Plays are different; the audience is hidden in the darkness and if you want, you can ignore them. But if you're making a speech, there's nowhere to hide. You don't know how disturbing it is when the entire audience won't stop looking at you.

Each time another name was called out, I broke into a sweat. I was tempted to scoot. What was the worst that could happen? I'd get a lecture from Pandarpattebai. So what? At least I wouldn't have to go through this. I had just taken my courage in my hands and was getting up when the student on stage finished his speech on 'My Favourite Bird' or some such and they called out, 'Swarupa Hemant Saraf'. My escape route closed with a clang.

I made my way to the topic basket and pulled out a slip. Five minutes on 'Our City'. Who set this topic? A mad man? How was I supposed to cover a city like Mumbai in five minutes? When I tried to think, I got even more worked up. Okay, some introductory remarks, then the major issues...but how many major issues there were! It was dizzying even trying to pick one.

My head began to spin. And then the time for thought had ended. I went blank. When I climbed on the platform, my head was close to empty. Not one of those thousands of issues would come into focus. Everyone was looking at me and my mouth was dry. So I simply opened it and began to speak.

~

Twenty-five years later, I can't remember what I said. I must have spoken well. I got the best marks in that round and I stood first in the finals which were held not long afterwards. All that I can remember is the dry mouth, the indecision and the ice-cold certainty that I was going to make a mess of it.

Everything, the atmosphere, the tension, is still clear in my head. The scene comes back whenever we have a SEVA meeting. No reason really. It's not as if we have our meetings in a small class or there are old teachers sitting in front of us. We find a free space in the middle of the slum and set up a makeshift stage by tying some tables together. We hang the loudspeakers on a bamboo stand and we're done. The free space is almost always in front of a public toilet, and the smell hangs over us and the crowd of people who have gathered there in the belief that we can get them out of the slum and into permanent homes. In terms of subject matter, however, what we say is not very different from 'Our City'. The slums, the urban infrastructure or lack of it, the housing problem, all these have been there for ages. What I am going to say today is just another version of that speech.

But what has changed is me. I am no longer that young girl, the Swarupa Saraf who stood in front of an audience, stitching sentences together frantically. Today I am Swarupa Karkhanis and I have a clear role to play in Mumbai's redevelopment scenario. My voice may be heard everywhere, from the newspapers to the State Legislature.

Last month, it was SEVA's sixth anniversary. You can have no idea how difficult life in a slum is unless you have lived there yourself and struggled with the builders who want the land, the politicians who are hand in glove with the builders and the goonda element that wants to control everyone. SEVA tries to keep its balance on this tightrope. From making the residents aware of their fundamental rights to making sure their names appear on the deeds and documents of ownership in the new buildings, we are with them at every step of the way. We offer direction; we provide whatever support is needed. This can be anything, from registering their rent receipts with the Municipality to getting them legal help and advice. There are other issues too. Protesting illegal structures and sponsoring research into infrastructure etcetera. There are few organizations like ours who engage so completely with no expectation of rewards. Few? If you don't count SEHAT, Premendra's pioneering NGO, then there's no one else I can see.

SEHAT. The name makes me feel nostalgic. We go back a long way. From the time I was a nobody. I had just finished degrees in civil engineering and sociology—subjects that bore little relationship to each other and I had done a little contract work with various NGOs just to wet my feet, as it were. Soon after that, I married Aniruddh. I wasn't the kind to sit at home after the wedding. I must give Aniruddh credit for that; he never opposed my working. But how much of this could be put down to his beliefs and how much to self-interest, I can't say. I don't blame him anyway. For even before we married, he had warned me that he had no intention of joining the rat race like other men but was going to be a 'struggler', an aspiring actor in Mumbai's phrasebook. He had done a few plays and television serials but it wasn't possible to survive on that kind of money. So one could argue that he didn't really have much option but to let me work. And it was around this time that I met Premendra. At the time, I was content with my lot but uncertain too, groping for direction.

Our first meeting was at a conference in Jaipur; almost overnight I was working at SEHAT. I liked Premendra—or at least his way of thinking—immediately. He had some brilliant new ideas about the direction Mumbai's progress should take. We became friends during this conference. Such good friends that Premendra's colleagues and his personal assistant, Ramnath, began to look at us with suspicion. But there was nothing physical about our attraction to each other. It might have had something to do with my tendency to develop strong loyalties, but I don't think I ever thought of it that way at the time. I think that Premendra may have noticed however. For he never once mentioned it, not even by implication. Our common passion was our desire to do something new and different. It was during those four days that he offered me the chance to work with him at SEHAT and I came back to Mumbai and put in my papers and joined. The organization was growing rapidly. Funds were pouring in. The very next month we'd signed up with Dorab Mistry Architects and Pune's Pant-Prabhu as builders and had started work on our most important project at Lokmanya Nagar.

This was when I met Sanika. She was working at Dorab Mistry's firm and we became firm friends. It didn't last, of course. Those halcyon days didn't last either. Maybe they were too good to last. But it was a time when I grew in self-confidence, I found my direction in life and I gained valuable experience, all kinds of domain knowledge, and an understanding of the responsibilities one has to take and the perhaps-inevitable political manoeuvring and betrayals.

I ignored the bitter aftertaste that these memories brought back and tried to refocus on the task at hand. It's never easy to push SEHAT away when it comes back. In this particular case, I even knew why I was thinking about it. The meeting at Sadavarte Nagar was bringing back those memories. For one thing, Sadavarte Nagar is right next to Lokmanya Nagar. When I parked the car, it was right outside the huge gates of Lokmanya Nagar and I thought back to the time Sanika and I would spend days and nights finalizing those drawings.

~

Right next to the gate, Nair was smoking. This is one of his habits that I do not care for. Perhaps it has something to do with my memories of Aniruddh. He loved smoking. He looked rather elegant, smoking. For him, the cigarette became a symbol of his rebellion against convention. But things change. I guess your past affects you in more ways than one.

'Good evening, ma'am,' Nair said and put out the cigarette, almost embarrassed. Then ignoring my annoyance, he said, 'Early today? It's just gone five. The meeting's at seven.'

'I know. Don't worry about it,' I said, coolly, surveying the thrown-away butt with displeasure. 'I'm just taking a round.'

But Nair wasn't there to listen. He had pulled out his cell phone and was talking to the sound system guys, warning them that I had arrived, telling them to get on with it and was leading the way to the meeting site.

To the average middle-class person, all slums look alike. The same overflowing gutters, the plastic or asbestos or plywood constructions, the same paan shop at a corner, the same illegal electric connections, the same video parlours and the stink of illegal liquor dens. But that isn't true. Each settlement has its own identity, its own culture, its own rules, its own ways of building, its own politics (which are never revealed early). To see these differences, you have to be ready to look for them…as I am.

Perhaps because of its proximity, Sadavarte Nagar has some of the markings of Lokmanya Nagar. So much so that as I walked through it, I began to feel a sense of nostalgia for a time when I was not burdened by a sense of responsibility but simply had a job to do. Happy days.

In those days, Sanika and I were totally involved with the project. We did much of the ground work of Lokmanya Nagar: talking to the people, showing them the designs and explaining them, coordinating with the consultants, all of it. Until I left SEHAT, this area had become a second home to me. I spent most of my time here and the rest either at the office of Dorab Mistry or at the BMC. During this time, I became pregnant. I was overjoyed though the happiness did not last. Soon Sanika's behaviour began to change. She began to stay away from work, using her ill health as an excuse. I took the load but I began to feel the strain. I tried to talk to Premendra about this a few times but he had other things on his mind. He began to spend much more time with politicians. As his name began to appear in papers, the old Premendra began to vanish. In his place a new, cunning, slick man appeared, one with whom a real conversation was impossible. Because he saw nothing beyond his own agenda. And then one afternoon, I fainted at the site.

That day, as always, Sanika was on leave. Dorab Sir had some doubts about the accuracy of a survey and wanted a report by evening. This could not be left to the surveyor; it had been his mistake in the first place. I was quite well for the first hour or so. Then it began to grow hot and I started to develop a headache. The site supervisor said, 'Go home. I'll finish up here,' but I was too sure of myself to listen. I kept at it until a moment came when the darkness swam up before my eyes.

When I came to, people had gathered. In a panic, the supervisor had called everyone he could think of. Someone brought me water, someone gave me coffee. In a while Aniruddh came to get me. Generally, he did not concern himself with my work but that day I could understand his irritation.

The next day, I spoke to Premendra about it. I thought he would understand my situation but the exact opposite happened. The doctor had recommended bed rest but Premendra refused to let me have it and there was no alternative but for me to leave SEHAT. All at once, everything that I had relied on was slipping away but what could I have done about it?

Once I left SEHAT, I did not return to Lokmanya Nagar. I tried not to think about those days, tried to erase those memories. Then Aavart was born. Not long afterwards, Aniruddh's affair came to light. The divorce, the depression that followed...things kept changing dramatically. The only thing that I clung to was my integrity. I made no compromises in my work, never chose the easy way out.

Today, whether anything or anyone else travels with me or not, I have my integrity.

When I started SEVA and discovered my identity, things began to look up. Now no one can touch me: not Sanika, the close friend-turned-betrayer; not Premendra, the boss who sacked me unfairly; not Aniruddh, the husband who abandoned me and a baby son. And I no longer wanted to be entangled in the coils of the past. When I was a nobody, these little hurts gave me a sense of being somebody. Now they seem a bit pointless. That may be why I called Sanika when I saw her the other day...without bothering about whether her behaviour at the time was justified or not. She seemed to feel liberated too. Now let's see what comes next.

~

The narrow lane turned right abruptly and ended in a large-ish chowk. A small stage had been put up on which a canopy flapped; in front, a low hill of stackable plastic chairs. Two little boys were unstacking chairs and were lining them up. Nair rushed off to help them while I hovered in the background.

Behind the makeshift canopy, a line of the eight-storeyed buildings of Lokmanya Nagar loomed. That it was now well-settled was evident from the drying clothes that hung out of the windows. I suddenly remembered how much rage this flapping laundry caused Sanika. According to her, these clothes destroyed the elevation the architects had worked so hard to create. She had wanted a clause inserted into the home-handover agreements by which the residents would be forbidden from hanging clothes out of the windows but that had not been practical. At least not with a slum redevelopment scheme like this one.

These people wanted homes to live in; they weren't really bothered about aesthetics. But who can explain this to these architects? Even after all these years her rage might not have unabated, who knows? After all, the lady is now partner at SNA architects. They have projects that will rewrite the Colaba skyline—Elena, for instance; and recently they've been on the cover of

Indian Architect & Builder. What more evidence does one need of their professional success? They probably insert a 'No drying clothes' clause in every contract! My mood lightened and I began to smile a little.

I wasn't even supposed to be at the meeting today. Of late, work has increased so much that I don't have the time. So I'd mentored some of my colleagues and got them ready to take these meetings. Nair and Chipalkatti have started conducting them independently now. I suspect Nair is even better than I am. That in itself is not surprising. I started working here as a social responsibility. However long I work here, I will always be the upper-class person with an outsider perspective. On the other hand, Nair has lived for several years in a slum. His father, an electrician, had come to Mumbai looking for work and had found a home there. He didn't earn much but he couldn't leave Mumbai either. When Nair gets on to the stage to talk about redevelopment, those days probably come back. Not surprising then that he brings more conviction to what he says than I do.

This was also a very preliminary meeting and it isn't the stage at which I choose to get involved. I generally turn up at the fourth or fifth meeting, when the usual suspects have been rounded up and specific issues can be addressed.

Today something compelled me to come. From the day I met Sanika and made my peace with her, I have been thinking about Lokmanya Nagar and without any real reason, I decided to come today. It seemed difficult to believe now that after the Lokmanya Nagar Project was completed no one ever paid attention to such a huge plot so close to it.

There must have been some problem or the other. Something like high-tension lines running inconveniently across the slum. Or some of the city's underground services that weren't deep enough to survive rebuilding. Whatever it was, it was to our benefit that it had been ignored for so long. Earlier, it would have gone to Premendra and SEHAT. I would not have been able to stand up to him. Things are different now. Now I have made a niche for myself and in the meanwhile Premendra has been trying to get into politics and has done some damage to his clean image.

Odd, how much we change over time. It seemed as if we believed that each thing we do has a finality to it. That each experience affects our point of view and determines the direction and behaviour in the future. Bullshit!

Nair had finished setting up the chairs and having sent one of the boys for tea, was sitting in the middle somewhere, chatting on his mobile phone. He got married few months ago, so he was probably talking to his wife or so it seemed from the way he was billing and cooing. I called Aavart. He had just returned from school and was watching television. I warned him that he had to finish his homework and gave the help instructions about dinner. It was getting close to the time of the meeting. The people had also begun to gather. I began to look at my notes though there wasn't much preparation to do. For the last six years, I have given the same speech at least twenty-five times. Not the identical speech but one very close to it. The slum would change, the number of people would change, the associated political colouring and the lumpens would change but the speech would not.

On one side of the mandap, a long, broad table had been set on the stage with many 250-ml Bisleri bottles placed on it. I sat down on one of the plastic chairs and opened a bottle and drank it down. I was about to open a second, when the chair next to me was dragged up and someone sat down on it.

I didn't pay much attention but then he said my name and I turned to look.

Premendra was sitting next to me.

'You've done well, Swarupa. I am proud of you.'

Premendra had his calculated smile on. It was simultaneously familiar and unfamiliar. When I was working with him it had seemed so reassuring. You felt as if it had been put on specially for you. But that hadn't lasted long. His agenda had begun to show through it. Then he stood for election as an independent candidate. When he was contesting, his posters carried an image of him smiling and that white slash had begun to disgust me. So I was not surprised by that smile. I realized that his presence here was no accident, that he must have something in mind.

'It's been far too long, hasn't it? You know, I am a great

admirer of your work,' he said in his deep baritone. This was not how he sounded in the beginning. It had been a thinner voice then, higher in pitch, but when he saw his career moving towards the political arena he began to change in small and subtle ways: the way he looked, the way he spoke and yes, even the way he behaved. He now sported a French beard, started using glasses and wearing khadi. By dint of hard work, he changed his voice too. While this was happening, we didn't notice but when you thought back to the original Premendra the changes became apparent. It wasn't just a superficial change, his personality changed too. How much he had changed! But why is that surprising? Haven't I changed as well?

'Your SEVA is doing well. You've got some important projects and everyone in the industry knows you,' he went on, the smile unchanged. 'But I'm not talking about your NGO per se. I am talking about your personal achievement. You come across as a strong, responsible person in your work, in your writing. I am really proud that you spent your formative years in SEHAT.'

He stopped and looked at me over his glasses. Perhaps he thought I would take his cue, forget the past and accept this gesture of friendship.

'That's enough. What do you want, Premendra? Why are you here?' I asked brusquely.

His face did not change. His expression did not change. Suddenly, I had no doubt that he had expected me to react like this. He let a few seconds pass.

I looked beyond him and I saw Nair and two or three

volunteers coming to the stage. Seeing Premendra, they stopped in their tracks. A few seconds later my mobile vibrated.

Nair's SMS: 'Everything ok?'

My reply: 'Sure. Give me 1 mt.'

'Premendra, in all the years since you sacked me from SEHAT on Sanika's say-so, you haven't so much as e-mailed me. I don't believe you're suddenly regretting what you did. So give me some credit and tell me what brings you here.'

'No, no, you're getting me all wrong.' Premendra protested. He took off his spectacles and began to play with them. 'What I did then was not wrong. I am not here to apologize. You think it was easy to let you go? It was a very tough decision. But at that point you and Sanika just could not have worked together. So much had happened between the two of you that keeping you both on was just impossible. Plus, you openly challenged my authority. Let it go now. Forget it. Tell me this: if you'd continued working with me, would you have got where you are now? In a way, I did you a favour!'

There was some truth to what he said but Premendra was never known to be stupid.

'Forget the past. Today I am here to ask you if you want to get even…'

'With you?' I still wasn't in the mood to listen.

Premendra laughed mischievously. Then he said, 'With me? Absolutely not! With Sanika.'

I looked at my watch. Fifteen minutes left to the

meeting. The crowd was gathering at its own pace. But there were also some unfamiliar faces which I had not seen in this area. Some were carrying laptop bags. Others had mics, not very efficiently concealed, behind their backs. Between the hutments, I could see an OB van on the road outside.

Reporters? What the hell! What was Premendra up to?

He wasted no time telling me. It was brilliant but it was a double-edged sword for me. For one, it made nonsense of the hand of friendship I had just extended to Sanika after so many years. It also meant I would become a pawn in a larger game Premendra was playing.

Now he put a file in front of me, a thin file. On the cover, in elegant lettering: Elena. Elena! SNA's flagship project.

I could feel Premendra's eyes on me. I let a few seconds pass before I picked up the file gingerly. For a moment I could not decide whether to open it or not. I had a feeling that I knew what it contained since Premendra was involved.

Finally, I did open it.

I was right. It was a ticking time-bomb. It listed all those who had helped getting that project up and going; who had broken what laws; who had removed the reserved tag from the property; who had increased the number of floors allowed...everything.

If this fell into the wrong hands it wasn't just Elena that wouldn't go up; many people would go down with it.

How he had got this information was no secret. There are enough people in this city who, for the right amount of money, will file Right to Information Act queries for others.

But that wasn't the important thing. The important thing was the next step.

I began to see what Premendra expected of me. It was a slippery slope. Once I set foot on it, there would be no turning back.

Elena had been in the limelight for a long time now. Colaba is full of heritage structures. So there isn't much space for big projects.

Elena was also noted for another reason. Among all the pseudo-Romantic structures which tried to look like heritage buildings, this clean-lined, well-designed building caught the eye. It was still under construction and that meant no one had seen what it would finally look like. But the promoters had been pushing it, so it was well known all over the city.

Sanika's firm had gained considerably from this project. The people who had booked the flats in it were rich and famous. Ordinary people wouldn't get a look in. There were film stars and industrialists who had bought into Elena. Their names were being used in the adverts. But what I was interested in, were the names that had not been used. Those other names; of relatives and friends, the names that had been suppressed.

Premendra's contact had dug out, from some other source entirely, a list of these hidden names, the people who had cleared the way for the project. And here it was, in front of me, a list, with evidence of how things had been changed from black to white. It was a clear accounting of how many rules had been broken or modified and who had taken the decision to do that and what they had gained from it. It was all here and once it came out, it would raise a humongous stink. There would be some hurried reassignments in Mantralaya and the Corporation. They would pretend to investigate the ministers who had signed off on the project but it would only be the heads of the less-important that would roll. And the architects who had signed the proposal? What would happen to them?

'I need time to think about this,' I mumbled. And I did. I needed time to put all this into perspective. Should I blow the lid off a scandal of this size just because Sanika had once made things difficult for me? I could not even guess how deep the roots of all this went. And I wasn't stupid enough to imagine that Premendra was doing all this just for my psychological well-being. There must be some self-interest involved, but since he was now neck-deep in politics, he wanted to shoot over my shoulder.

'This has to happen now. At this meeting,' Premendra said clearly, his voice carrying a new edge. 'You don't have to do much. You just talk about the land crisis in Mumbai and then mention Elena. Leave the rest to the press. I understand your dilemma but time is a luxury we can't afford. Wheels are already turning. And in another day or two, we won't be able to control anything.'

Premendra's phone began to ring and he put it on 'silent' and turned it to face me.

'Look. Already they're trying to silence me. If I take even one call from them, my hands will be tied. And then I won't even be able to tell you anything.'

I didn't bother to ask who 'they' might be.

~

On that day, on that stage, I began to feel as if I were back in the elocution competition, at the Pandarinath Thorat Guruji School. Premendra had given me a new topic, one I'd never expected to find in the basket. Would it be right to bring up Elena or would it be a mistake? There was no question of preparing. It had to be extempore. In its own way, this was a competition too.

Who wins? Who scores?

To win now, to win today, that is the only truth. The rest is all a lie.

While there was much to say, I found my mind going blank. As the first two or three speakers were going on with their trivial matters, the debate continued inside my head: To mention Elena or not? And if I were to mention it, was the reason for doing that right or wrong? I would be exposing a huge scam but was I doing so for the greatest common good? Or had my forgiving Sanika been superficial? Was I still harbouring a grudge against Premendra for sacking me? And were I to do the right thing for the wrong reasons, what difference remained between me and Premendra? And most importantly, what of the integrity on which I pride myself?

But there was no getting away now. At any moment, my name was going to be called. The press was ranged in front of us with their paper pads and other devices at the ready. Sitting in front of me, Nair was perplexed to see the new lines springing up on my forehead. Premendra, having done his work, had vanished. It was time to make a decision. Thousands of muddled questions bumped through my head but otherwise it was empty. All the issues which had been clamouring for attention vanished. All eyes were on me and the flashbulbs had begun to go off. But still my head was empty. I couldn't even choose to run, an option I had thought of using in that classroom. I would have to play this game. And so I decided that I would play. The time for thinking was over.

It was the time for action.

I opened my mouth and began to speak.

~

I have always felt that when someone says, 'I'm doing this for the greatest common good' it's only a way of saying, 'I'm going to do what I want to do'. As long as you can put it down to the best interests of society in general, it does not matter whether you've betrayed a friend, harmed a community, anything. There may be some residual discomfort but 'the greatest common good' will make it possible for you to sleep at night.

Or so I thought.

But that night after Aavart fell asleep, I found myself on the balcony with no easy answers. I could hear the sound of breaking news on the television in the other room.

I was trying to figure out how to answer all the missed calls. I was preparing the answers and then scrapping them and starting over again and again. What would I see in the newspaper in the morning? I didn't want to play this new competitive game where victory is as bad as defeat.

Now the days of sleeping peacefully were over.

Perhaps forever.

JUMP

From where I was sitting, I could see the sea. Far away. Really far away. Which means, if I were to go down, get out the car, and drive, it would take roughly an hour or an hour and a half to get there. That's taking into account the 5:30 p.m. fuck-all traffic. But that's no surprise. When you're going from Point A to Point Anywhere in Mumbai, you've got to take the traffic into account.

Anyway, the sea. From here, it looks a little pathetic, framed by buildings on both sides. There is the island of the Haji Ali mosque too. In the heat and dust of this city, it shines in the warm light of the evening. The fun of it is the sun is directly overhead. The rain may begin at any moment now. The sun over Haji Ali isn't concerned about the threat of rain. It shines, lost in its own world. On the other side of the sea-face, the new stadium is visible. It catches the eye because of its peculiarly designed dome. The area beyond it is like some weird urban design experiment. Two cities stand side by side, resolutely refusing to converse with each other: the old Mumbai and the new one that wants to compete with

Singapore. Even if you stare, you can't tell where one ends and the other begins. For an architecture student like me, this is very interesting. Almost like witnessing the death and the rebirth of the city. In one glance, I can take in a few last remaining two- and three-storey buildings of Parel-Lalbaug, the ruins of the mills that have been closed down, a few eight- and ten-storey buildings of the middle period when FSI was relaxed a little, once seemingly huge but in comparison to the monsters of today, almost invisible.

Those monsters, all glass grins and concrete teeth, have eaten up the sky, each one blotting out a little more of my sea view, but how can I complain? I live in just such a monster, in one of the three or four flats Dad has bought as investments.

And anyway, I'm not here for the long run.

No way, José.

I tapped the ash off my cigarette and tossed the empty. Then my phone, which I had placed on the parapet, rang.

'Ramya, is that you?' Harsh was squeaking.

Harsh: classmate, from school and now in architecture school. Harmless sort. Well brought up, well meaning. Panics easily. From his voice, panic was happening.

'Ramya, answer me, are you there?'

'You called me, right?' I tried to calm him down.

'Your text just now. What did you mean?' Harsh's voice was getting higher.

'Was it not clear? "I'm tired of it all"? It was meant to be a suicide note. Or a suicide text.' I said and up to that point I kept my calm. 'But what did you think? I sent you the text and then immediately went and jumped? Be reasonable, man!'

I did my best imitation of a sane person. Then I looked down.

No one had gathered yet. That's Mumbai for you. Everyone has something to do. Whether anyone else lives or dies or is going to die or seems to be about to die, they don't have the time. Now shouldn't someone have noticed me, sitting on the parapet of a twenty-three-storey building, dangling his feet in the cool evening air? But who has the time? Had I pulled this stunt in a decent city like Nashik or Pune, a gratifying number of people would have gathered by now. Mumbai? Such a spoilsport. If someone were really trying to kill himself, he would have been miserable. I almost felt happy that I had no intention of doing something that stupid. I was just trying to get into the spirit of things.

'Where are you?' Harsh was in no mood to listen.

'At home. Where else?' I swung my legs over the edge and got down on the terrace. Without an audience, what's the point of sitting here?

'No, you're not. I called you on your landline.'

See? That's why I told Dad I don't need a landline.

'Arre… I was sleeping. My cell was on a side table.'

'Don't tell lies.'

What can I say? He knows me too well. But then again, if he did, he should have known I was joking.

'I'm on my way. Be there in ten. Should I call Riddhi?'

'Arre, why call Riddhi? She has nothing to do with this.'

'Okay. I'm coming. Don't do anything stupid,' Harsh shouted in my ear.

'Depends on your definition of stupid, right?' I said with a laugh.

'You know what I mean,' he said and hung up.

I could see Harsh in a panic, buttoning his shirt as he ran out of the house, thundering down the steps, ignoring the lift. Luckily, his car has just got back from the garage. In his excited state, I can't imagine him trying to find a cab. But in his excited state driving might also be a problem.

Whatever. His problem. Not mine.

Waiting for Harsh, I thought about calling Riddhi but it made no sense. It wasn't even four days that I'd broken off with her against her wishes. Actually, I enjoyed her company but it was getting too serious for me. Anyway, what's done is done. Now there's no going back. Even if there were, what would she do here?

The first drops of rain hit and I ran into the shelter. I really hate this shelter. The space between its four pillars is narrow and the pyramidal roof, disproportionate. I cannot believe how so-called landscape designers can use such hackneyed features. It's a waste. Just think: if you have come up on the terrace for a breath of fresh air, why would you huddle under one of these? Is it even likely? Okay, there are moments like this one but these are rare. And who would come out here in the rain? Wouldn't a sane person take his mug of coffee—or beer as the case may be—and sit in his balcony? Which is what I ought to be doing. Now even the magnificent Haji Ali sun had acknowledged defeat and, from the terrace, I could see nothing beyond a kilometre or so. And the rain was coming down now, in earnest.

I went down and got a fresh cigarette out of the pack and lit it, with the rough-and-ready gas lighter. And then I closed the doors and windows and put some old sobfest music on the Bose system. I put two mugs full of water into the microwave and perched on the counter, smoking. By the time Harsh arrived, the coffee would be ready.

You have to understand one thing if any of this is to make sense. People say I feel nothing, care for nothing and in a way, they're right. I'm not terribly keen on this emotion thing. It's a waste of time. That doesn't mean I don't like to play with emotions. It's good fun. You should try it sometimes. Of course, I don't do it all the time. No one would believe it. And then what would be the point? Today too I wasn't going to try anything. But my parents have been screwing my head so much, I really needed some cheering up. Harsh's panic attack had been worth it. Now I'm almost back to normal.

'What the fuck, Ramya? What the fuck?' Harsh's opening lines.

I took a gulp of coffee. Sugar. I should have added some sugar. I thought for a moment and then decided against it. Dad has severe diabetes. So the family doctor insisted that I should take care, even at this stage. In his words, 'The signs aren't good.'

'You frightened the shit out of me. I saw your text and thought you'd already…you know.'

'That's nothing. I was just pulling your leg.'

'Fuck you,' Harsh started forward and pushed me. The coffee in my hand splashed around and some fell on the dhurrie. 'How can you say that? Don't say these things casually. I've told you a thousand times. Now that you've expressed the idea, it's out there. Now it's a possibility, something inside your head. You won't be able to erase it.'

'Rubbish.' With that vote of confidence, I took Harsh to the living room. He cradled his coffee as he lowered himself into my big cappuccino beanbag and I went and stood at the door of the balcony.

The sea and everything else, the design experiment of the city included, had vanished. Now it could be any city, from New York to Hong Kong, glittering in the night. The lights of the city had filled up the darkness in front of the building.

Harsh has 'theories'; this is one of them. When Purandare and Monisha from our class broke up, he said the same thing. Purandare and Monisha were much in love. Everyone thought they would stay that way. Next stop marriage, children, right up to the retirement home. But once Monisha said she didn't plan to stick around forever, Purandare got nervous. All this went down in our canteen, with us and fifty-odd students present. I was wasting time with a cutting chai. Riddhi was actually at a lecture and other than waiting for her, we didn't have much else to do. I remember clearly how Monisha marched angrily out of the canteen. And immediately, Harsh said, setting his tea down, 'It's over.'

I called him a fool. I said that a single fight wasn't going to end things. We could all see how much they loved each other.

But Harsh was confident.

He didn't think love had much to do with it. When an idea is inside your head, he maintains, it has no weight; it's just a figment of your imagination. But as soon as you say it to someone, it acquires a life of its own. If Purandare and Monisha had decided to break it off inside their individual heads but had never said anything, they might have been able to put it together again. But now it was said and so it had to be.

I don't pay much attention to Harsh's babbling; but the funny thing is that it was actually over, just like that. They patched up in the evening but the idea just remained there. Neither could forget it. And after the Diwali vacation, Harsh was right.

Or was he?

In other words, I don't believe that if it holds true for Purandare and Monisha, it would hold for me. So if he thought I'd get worried, it wasn't going to work. It might have been an issue if I had said all this seriously. This Harsh won't get. So he's going to stay worried. And for now, he may be convinced but he will continue to believe that I am depressed at some subconscious level. This will be his new theory.

'...giving it, right?' I got the last few words of a sermon Harsh had been giving. I had to conceal the fact that I had been paying no attention, so I grabbed at the easiest response.

'Y...es but what's the hurry?' I said, trying to make out what he was trying to say with no context.

Harsh looked at me suspiciously.

'Did you even hear what I said?' he asked.

I looked at him blankly.

Caught.

'Sorry,' I said. He had known it all along.

'I asked: you all right, no? Submissions on time and all that?'

'Oh yeah. What shit you ask. I thought you wanted Dad's cell phone number or something.'

He laughed incredulously. 'In case you're forgetting, I have his number.'

Naturally. What was I thinking? When I'd had enough of Dad's messes, I left home and spent some time at Harsh's. Before I came here. In his usual organized fashion, Harsh had saved all my emergency numbers. Naturally he had Dad's number.

'And what's more, I've called him here,' Harsh said victoriously.

That took the wind out of my sails. I flopped down into the only easy chair in the room.

'Are you okay, Ramya?' Harsh seemed genuinely

concerned, but what was the point of this genuine concern? Maybe he'd thought Dad would calm me down or something. How would he know that Dad was the reason I was in this state?

So I explained the problem in detail. Harsh knew that my dad was sleeping around with these sordid starlets he met since his firm was financing some B-grade shit films. Which is why I find it impossible to stay in the same house with him. Even so, maybe Harsh thought that my mum's return meant things had improved. In reality, ever since she's returned it's become impossible to even visit them, never mind live in the same house. They just fight all the time. I get daily reports from my building buddies. Things are not good at all.

So it helped improve my mood a little that Dad hadn't even called for quite a while. Then the intercom buzzer sounded. It was time to move. Harsh was about to pick up the phone when I pulled him back and shoved my feet into my slip-ons.

By the time we legged it back up, twenty minutes had passed. Since it was past 8 p.m., the terrace would be closed by security. Unfortunately, the security guard, whom I keep happy with a regular supply of cigarettes, was missing in action. So I had to run down and find another guard.

When I got to the ground floor, Dad was making a scene in the security office. Harsh's phone call had done the trick. He probably feared what Harsh had feared. I just don't get these people. On the one hand, they say I don't give a shit. On the other, they think I'm sensitive enough to do something drastic like committing suicide. I could hear Dad demanding they open the door with the spare key. But the manager had gone home and no one knew where the spare keys were. A right royal mess. So we decided to hide in the terrace lobby and hopped it. Luckily, the lift was in the lobby. To throw them off track, we got off three floors early and ran up the rest. Then both our phones began to ring. We put them both on silent and kept on running. We were out of breath by the time we got to the terrace.

There was only one light on in the terrace lobby. Energy-fucking-conservation. They waste electricity in the stupidest of places and where it's needed, they practice conservation. Idiots! Both of us flopped into a chrome-and-leather sofa and whooshed out breaths…

Then we leaned back and took out our phones. The missed calls on both our phones were from Dad. I checked my messages and was about to log into Facebook when Harsh said, 'I think the terrace is open.'

'What?' I said, not looking up. 'Not possible. Society rules. Closed after eight. Silly, but it is what it is.'

'Take a look,' he said and before I could, he got up and went to the door.

I was about to bring an 'I-told-you-so' expression to my face when he got to the door and gave it a shove. A gust of cold night air flowed in. No light on out there. This was decidedly odd.

Harsh turned to me with a shrug. I motioned him

to stop and ran forward. The single light of the lobby reached about ten feet outside, in an elongated rectangle determined by the door frame. Outside of that, darkness. Zero visibility.

'Someone forgot to lock it,' Harsh whispered in a conspiratorial tone and began to look for the torch app on his phone.

'Don't be an asshole. They'd lose their jobs if some kids came up to play and fell off. Someone *opened* this door,' I said.

There was no real reason to whisper. Our opening the door would have signalled our entry on to the terrace. She or he—I'm not sexist—would have looked our way immediately, or so I thought.

I saw the spark of the cigarette first and then slowly, the outline of the man. He was sitting with his back against one of the pillars of the shelter. Was he drunk? When we walked up, he came to with a start.

'Hi,' he said.

'Hey.'

Long pause.

'I know who you are,' he murmured, almost as if thinking aloud. 'Not by name perhaps but I've seen you around.'

I shrugged. No shit, Sherlock! I live here. Then I realized that he wouldn't have seen me shrug. But he had recognized me in the darkness, which was quite surprising. Perhaps he'd spent so much time there, his eyes had grown accustomed to the dark. Or he'd got a quick glimpse of my face in the light of Harsh's cell phone torch.

'No kidding,' I said for something to say.

'No, no kidding,' he said. 'I saw you earlier. Up here.'

Earlier? Here? In the middle of the suicide fantasy? Fuck.

Harsh frowned.

'When?' he asked, fear in his voice.

'An hour or so ago?'

'Very likely,' I tried to cover up. 'I did come up for a stroll. But no one was here.'

'Not when you came. I arrived after you,' he said. 'When I came I saw you with your legs hanging over the edge. In a brown study. I thought you were ready to jump.'

I laughed and mumbled something like, 'Don't be ridiculous,' but the damage was done. Harsh was terrified. Whoever this guy was, he'd dumped me in a soup. Now even if I were to say, 'I was only joking,' no one was going to believe me. I could already see sympathy in his eyes. I hate pity more than anything else. When I think about it, that's probably the main reason I pushed Riddhi away: she insisted on feeling sorry for me. 'Poor Ramya. His father's in the middle of this awful scandal. And his mother abandoned him to run off to Australia when he was a boy…so sad! So what if his dad's loaded?'

What she called love was nothing more than sympathy. Fuck it. Harsh goes next or so it seems. I don't need friends. Not like these anyway.

But that was for later. At that point, I wanted to know who that guy was and what his problem was.

'Sorry. We haven't been properly introduced. I'm Ramakant. I live in 21B. This is Harsh, friend of mine. And you are?' I said and offered my hand. On cue, Harsh shone a torch on his face.

'No one you know,' he said and stuck his hand up to break the beam of light. But in that second, I got a good look and saw that it was a familiar face. Where had I seen him? College? Dad's office? Somewhere else? In an architecture firm where I'd interned in the vacations? This last was a definite possibility. Each vacation I had interned somewhere or the other. Correa, Kadri, SNA, Panthaky…you name it. One of these, certainly.

SNA? I was almost positive about this last one but his name still eluded me.

Anyway, no time to be talking now. Finding a place to go to ground was first priority. Finding the flat empty and the car in the parking lot, it would not take Dad long to track me down here. Or up here. It didn't make much sense to be sitting here, talking like this in the open.

'We're going to hide behind the lift room. You won't tell anyone, right?' Harsh asked, flashing his torch in the man's eyes.

'No. Actually, I was leaving myself. No point sitting here doing nothing, is there?' he said.

'Sorry,' I couldn't help it. 'What were you doing here again?'

'Nothing really. What you were doing earlier, I suppose…thinking.'

'Finished thinking?'

But then we heard the sound of the lift and we ran. We concealed ourselves behind the lift room and all the lights went on, one after the other, and then the cackle of concerned folk.

Ten minutes later, we were out of there.

I tried to ask my mole who the guy was but they hadn't seen anyone. Smart guy. He'd disappeared into thin air.

~

The next two or three hours went in us listening to Dad's lectures. Both of us got it: I because of my general bad behaviour and ingratitude; and Harsh because he didn't take Dad's calls and ran with me. You may have heard of Kübler-Ross' five stages that people facing death go through. Any of Dad's arguments would have fit roughly into one of these.

Denial: 'This is just not happening, Ramya.'

Anger: 'How could you do this, Ramya?'

Bargaining: 'What will it take to stop you doing this, Ramya?'

Depression: in which his face sagged.

Acceptance: in which he threw up his hands.

So predictable as to be almost silly.

But that day he just wouldn't stop shouting. Thankfully, the windows in my apartment are soundproof or the neighbours would have heard it all. The odd thing was that what he was saying actually made sense this time.

So if he had spoken to me quietly, there would have been a better chance that I'd have listened to him. If he was telling the truth, then the shouting and the fighting between him and Mom was their way of working things out. He was delighted to have her back. He had come here when Harsh called him, not because he was afraid I might do something but just to warn me in person that he had had it with my stupid pranks.

When he left, Harsh and I sat there, unsure of what to think. I took out a cigarette, opened the sliding doors, the windows. I was leaning on the rail and looking down. Harsh came out with a pair of Buds. I thought about what Dad had said as I looked at the lights of the city and the dark spaces where the sea could no longer be seen. However, it was not I but Harsh who spotted the crowd that had now gathered below.

You might ask: what can you see from the twenty-first floor? You'd be surprised at the detail one can see. Even now, two police jeeps, an ambulance and the elders and gawkers who had gathered were clearly visible. And the crowd was growing denser. Just as we were beginning to wonder what happened, my phone rang.

Dad.

'Do you know anyone called Partho Sengupta? He was with SNA. You interned with them in your second year, if I'm not mistaken.'

Oh shit. That's where I'd seen him, the guy on the terrace. What had remained in my memory was his typical Bengali name. Also his Brahmin style, his accent-free, chaste Marathi and the intriguing combination thereof. He must have made quite an impression for me to remember him.

'What happened to him?' I asked for the sake of asking. Because I knew. Disappearing into thin air is never easy. I came inside and leaned against the wall.

'He just jumped from your terrace an hour or two ago. Did you know him?'

As if on cue, the rain began to hammer down, rumbling, thundering and the shining lights outside began to go out, one by one, and gusts came in through the open doors of the balcony.

But in that moment, I was not aware of any of this. I stood there, watching Harsh hopping about to close doors and windows, still pressing the phone to my ear.

Did the whole thing make any sense? I just didn't know.

~

Thinking about it later, two odd things stood out.

The first was that in the dark, in a new and unfamiliar context, after two years, I had still recognized Partho. I pride myself on my good memory, of course, but this was a stretch. I had been at SNA for about three months and since I was in the second year I didn't even do any significant work. At SNA, he was in the liaison gang. We hardly ever met them. No regular contact. I didn't even know Partho had come to live here. And yet I recognized him immediately.

Not by name but so what?

Smart, right?

The other: Harsh's theory. Once expressed, the idea is out there. Of course, he had said it about me. In other words, once I said it, it became a realistic probability for me, or something like that. But in this case, even if it wasn't about me, that is about what happened, right? I thought it up, I sat on the parapet but that fantasy became a reality. A possibility for Partho.

Don't get me wrong. I don't think I'm responsible for his suicide. Like Renoir said, 'The truly terrible thing is that everybody has their reasons'. But if he hadn't seen me sitting like that, would he have thought of it?

Would he have found the courage? Who knows?

Life is funny like that, if you know what I mean.

FLOOD

IT WAS PAST SEVEN WHEN I CROSSED THE HAJI ALI STRETCH. The traffic was insane and the rain wasn't helping. No one would believe it had been nice and hot not so long ago. Visibility outside the car was about five feet. The wipers, on at full speed, gave me a second to see and then the veil of rain fell again. The FM radio channel was doing its best to scare people, resurrecting the flood of 26 July 2005. That's their game: terrifying the populace. Nothing like that was going to happen today. But it would be nice to get a day off.

I looked at my watch again for no real reason. The hands hadn't moved much; nor had the cars. I had just finished a meeting for a new project. Actually, there's no real reason to go back to the office. It'll take at least an hour. And even when I get there, it's not as if we'll get anything accomplished. But who's to convince Agashe? He's the boss. What he says goes. It isn't as if I didn't try. I sent him an SMS. But no. He wanted me there. Now. Ridiculous.

By the time I fought through the sluggish traffic and reached office, it was 8:15 p.m. I'm not like, 'I'm never in the office past eight' or anything like that, right? I mean, like all other offices in Mumbai, our timings are erratic too. But to come back to the office in this downpour...I mean, really!

Agashe is so unreasonable sometimes. I like him the least of our three bosses. Now, don't get me wrong. He is usually considerate but with everything that's going on in the office, anyone might go haywire. Oddly, this has made Sanika even more cool and precise than usual. I like her. She's principled and meticulous. But I'm stuck in the dungeons with Agashe.

As his PA, I am always with him. Ironically, that means I get more free time in our office than anyone else. And I also get to spend time with Partho as a bonus. Partho is Agashe's blue-eyed boy. The two of them handle liaison for our projects which seem to increase by the day. So there are lots of one-on-one or two-on-one which I can skip. But the past four-five days have been anything but normal.

If you read the newspapers, you'll know what I'm talking about. These days we're all over the press. And we're in damage control mode.

~

By the time I reached office, it was deserted. Almost everyone had finished and left for the day. Today that's justifiable. It's been raining like mad for some time. My teeth began to chatter as I entered the office—not from the temperature—but because I was wet. This is a major problem with our office. No parking. We do have our spaces in the stilt area but all three of those are for the bosses; Sanika never uses her car so hers is on standby for clients. Sometimes Partho gets to use that one. Since he works with Agashe on all the doings and dealings at the BMC, he has a hold on the partners. But for me there was nothing to do but to circle around hunting for space. Now that it was after office hours, it should be easier. As I expected, I found a spot quite soon, but three buildings away. The water was beginning to gather. Despite my umbrella, I was drenched. When I got into the building, of course, the fourth space was empty.

I was actually hoping to meet Partho at the office. But today of all days, he'd vanished. Normally he's one of the last to leave. Which explains his blue-eyed boy status. Today he seems to have broken the rule and he didn't even tell me. So no one seemed to be around. I dropped my bag off at my workstation and as I pushed open a door of the pantry to see if the coffee machine was working, I almost bumped into Sanika. To my 'Good evening', she mumbled, 'Evening Nita' as she went out.

Normally, she stops and talks, but today she seemed preoccupied, even gloomy. No surprise there. I had forwarded her the flight tickets to Seattle. I didn't even get a chance to ask if she'd seen them. But under the circumstances, who could blame her? The question is whether she can go to Seattle now. It's not a fortnighter; it's for six months. But perhaps she'll just have to go. The Rednecks Group project needs her to jumpstart it. And with Elena on the boil, we can't afford to take risks with any of our existing clients. She'll have to go whether she wants to or not.

Generally, if I'm called in this late, it's because there's some big meeting planned. Someone from Agashe's VIP list is showing up at the office. Since I'm Agashe's PA, I have no choice but to stay even though everyone else is free to make a break for it. Generally, I have no role to play in these meetings; it's just a matter of protocol. Today is no exception. But anyway, whoever is or isn't around, Partho should have been here. Handling these messes is part of his job. I haven't even seen him in the last four or five days; almost from the point when it hit the fan. Today, he should have really been here. I had sent him a message earlier but there was no reply. Could the rain have jammed the signal? Was he stuck in the rain or had he reached home? Because it's raining like crazy now. Ever since I got in, it's just gone haywire. From the narrow pantry window, the chunk of prime real estate we can normally see has started vanishing. The double glazing is thrumming with the rain, a sound as regular and meaningless as radio static. This wouldn't be 26 July replaying itself, would it?

~

By the time I was filling the second cup of coffee, I was feeling much better. I took my cup to the reception and called Dad. He thought I was going out for dinner with Partho as usual. We haven't made an official announcement yet, but Dad knows. I think he likes Partho; otherwise it doesn't take him long to announce his opposition. I told him that I was in the office, sitting at the reception. He knows how it goes so he just said, 'Okay, but try to come home quickly. And drive carefully.'

Kajal, our receptionist, has it good. She got married a few months ago so she leaves on the dot. She gets here at nine and she's out at six. You say something and she tears up. In comparison, I appreciate Sanika's commitment. Agreed Sanika hasn't married, but she's been in a relationship for a while and I've never known her to say, 'I have to leave by this time' or 'I can't stay past this time'. Of course, you can't compare Sanika and Kajal. Sanika is one of bosses; she can't afford to complain.

I picked up my coffee and sat down in Kajal's chair. In front of me, SNA's logo—a new one, a big one, chrome-plated. A cool font. S for Sanika, N for Niranjan—that's Agashe—and A for Anant, or as Sanika will have it, Antya. Now it seems odd but when I joined, I thought the A stood for 'Associates' and the 'Architects' was stuck on afterwards merely as information. Turned out I was wrong. But if a man is called Antya, how are you to guess he's a partner? In the first few days, I was going to make the faux pas of calling him Antya but then Partho saved me in time. That was when we began to become real friends. Antya is a name only Sanika is privileged to use, from their college days together. Agashe calls him Anant or goes to the extent of 'Anant Sir' sometimes.

Actually, Anant does look very smart, real boss material. Of the three, he's the best turned out. Agashe is damn dominating; Sanika looks like a college kid. All three don't like formality. We use 'Sir' and 'Ma'am' when we are in meetings or on site but otherwise it's all first-name basis. I think Sanika has a complex. She likes to think she looks much younger than she is. It's clear from the way she dresses and make no mistake, she puts a lot of thought into her clothes. Never mind if it doesn't work.

Apart from the logo, it's the model of Elena that dominates the reception space. Elena: up until recently, our biggest project and right now, our biggest headache. You can't imagine how quickly it changed from one to the other. The work was going on in full swing. Approvals were in place, the slabs were going up at the right pace, the design decisions had been made. We were even a couple of weeks ahead of schedule. But last week that Karkhanis female from the NGO Whatsit began to babble about corruption and political will and everything went bust.

Now you tell me, where isn't there corruption? I agree the law should not be broken, but when the laws are so stringent that you can't do a thing without breaking them, what then? Aren't all projects built on the basis of some injustice? And as far as Elena went, it wasn't as if we ripped off some Adivasis, stole tribal land or drove out some slum-dwellers. It was just a matter of greasing some palms along the way, pure and simple. As clean as it could be made. So why did this NGO have to stick its nose in? If they wanted money, they should have said so. With such a big project and so many zeroes involved, you can move a few figures from one column to another and no one will even notice. But no, they just want to cause trouble. If they see some progress happening, they start to burn. They don't seem to have heard of the greater common good.

Up to now we'd had such a good run on Elena and then at some slum-type meeting, this Karkhanis female lobbed her bomb and the channels were all over it.

And what else would they do? When you have twenty-four-hour news channels, is it a joke to run them? Breaking news, interviews, discussions, audience polls, they've got to have them all, or how are they going to feed the beast? They need news, to create the illusion that something is happening. And about Elena there was plenty to talk about. Before those slum people had even got home from the meeting, this Karkhanis female had become a TV star. That's what these people want. And Partho told me that Sanika and this Karkhanis female have some history. Which is why she caused this mess. He doesn't know all the details but there it is.

~

I clearly remember the day it all started. Partho and I had gone to TGIF's for an early dinner. They generally play sports channels but maybe there were no games that day or something because they had a Hindi news channel going. On mute. Now that's a joke, right? A news channel on mute? But that's how it was. So we'd ordered and we were chatting away happily about this and that when Partho's face went white. I turned and there was Elena. And underneath it the ticker tape had all the names from the Home Minister right up to Niranjan Agashe. We got the remote from the manager and tried changing the channel but to no avail, it was on all the channels. So we turned up the sound and listened. We heard that this Karkhanis female had been speaking at some random slum redevelopment meeting and she'd suddenly dragged up the Elena backstory and talked about how it was all a scam and she had the documents to prove it.

What more do the channels need? They began to scream. But what I found odd was something else entirely. From what they said on the news, it had been one of those routine slum meetings. That too an evening meeting. So how did that footage turn up as the lead story on every channel so quickly? Unless… I tried this one out on Partho but he was so shaken by the news, he couldn't think. That was but natural. Whatever building proposal we send out, Partho was next in line. After Agashe, of course. It was natural for him to feel responsible. We didn't stop to eat. We came out and called Agashe.

Since then, we've been on a roller-coaster ride. We were on every channel; there were editorials; we were the peg on which to hang all the problems of politics and the Municipal Corporation. Naturally, temperatures went up and the clients began to call in a panic…

God! Now I had to be in the office up to 9:30 or 10 p.m. If this goes on I'll have to start packing an overnight case.

Partho took the worst of it. Meaning, he kept up a cool front but I could tell his mind was working overtime. He was blaming himself. He would talk about Agashe as well. I couldn't see why he was so bothered if Agashe wasn't? And why should they be bothered in the first place? Means, they were all part of a large machine, right? If they wanted to get the job done, they had no choice.

I remember a professor we had in the second year: Sukhatme was his name, a brilliant man. A learned man, with marvellous design skills. He had worked with many institutions. But in his entire life he had never built so much as a fifty-square-foot room. He would often say: designing is not enough. You can do what you like on paper or on your computer but when you try to build, that's when you have to be able to fight it out in the real world. If you can do that, you're a real architect. I thought it was just frustration but he had a point. SNA proved it to me. I told Partho this but he seemed to be deep inside himself. He actually seemed more worried than Agashe even. I can understand why. He had been with Agashe for the last seven or eight years and Agashe has a very high opinion of Partho's abilities. Since our proposals are signed by Agashe, he is the one who is going to be in the worst soup.

But Agashe is always one of the smartest guys in

the room. He knows how to handle things. If he's not worried, I don't know why Partho is so het up. But that's Partho; he's not going to calm down.

~

When I looked at my watch, it was about to strike nine. It didn't seem like anyone would be coming for a meeting now. So why had they called me? No point asking Agashe though. He is very secretive and rarely answers. But if he called me, there must be something. I was wondering whether to go to my workstation when the phone rang.

Now? So late?

'SNA,' I said.

'Hi. Is that Kajal?' someone asked, his voice uncertain.

'Nita. Who is this?'

One of Kajal's old boyfriends? And even if it were, at this odd hour? I was partially right. It was a voice from the 'Boyfriend' category but not Kajal's.

'Nita? Hi. I think we have met in the office. This is Sushrut. Is Sanika in?'

Sushrut is Sanika's friend—or partner—or whatever the hell they call lovers these days. Cute sort. No airs. But why call on the board, not on her cell? Then he answered my unspoken question: 'Sorry to bother you, but Sanika's cell is switched off. I tried her direct line but that isn't connecting either. Is she there?'

Strange.

Sanika's number is never ever switched off.

And the direct line must be working. Or is the rain doing its number on the landlines?

'Yeah, she's there. Please hold.' I said and transferred the line. Engaged.

'Engaged,' I told Sushrut, frowning. 'Should I ask her to call you?'

'Please,' he said and hung up and I went in.

Our office has a strange layout. Or at least I found it strange at first. In most offices, the bosses' area and the staff area are clearly marked off from each other. Either the bosses are near the reception or deep inside in some isolated area. In our office, all three bosses have a common cabin...right in the middle of the staff area. If you take a couple of steps from the reception, you can see it.

On one wall is a huge screen for presentations under which there are some storage units. The other three sides are glass. The table isn't the typical cabin furniture either. It's a circular conference table, a six-seater. I have never seen all three bosses in the cabin at the same time; of course, there's a first time for everything. That day they were all in the cabin together.

When I set foot in the staff area, I knew something was wrong. Outwardly, everything seemed fine. But there are moments when you know instinctively that something's amiss. Some of the staff areas were well-lit. One of these was around my workstation where I had put on the lights, tick-tick-tick, when I came in. The other two areas were where Sanika's staff sit. Other than these, everything else was in darkness. Where I sit, there's a long line of windows. But since the office is wide, the light doesn't penetrate the whole area even during the day, never mind at this time of night.

The cabin was a little further away. All the halogen spots were on. Sanika was sitting at the table, her back to me. Anant was standing next to her and talking. It looked like he was explaining something to her. Agashe was leaning on the storage unit, calm as always. The usual Elena loop was playing on the telly; the usual rehash of what was known, the usual montage of images. Each channel uses the same stuff with minor tweaking: Elena in various stages of being built, shots of old Mumbai and those of the new skyscrapers, our offices, the photo of the bosses that had appeared on the cover of a magazine recently, and a clip of Agashe pushing a reporter out of the way when they had all gathered outside the office on the second day of the whole tamasha.

Some anchor was going over the old stuff behind the images but it didn't seem as if even one of them was listening. And since I was in relative darkness outside the cabin, perhaps I couldn't be seen either. At least so it seemed. Because when I knocked all three of them jumped, the way actors do in films or plays. Why, I wondered idly. Because they had momentarily thought no one was in the office? Because of the half-darkness outside? Because they had all been thinking so deeply that they couldn't see me?

When I went in, they looked worried. It didn't suit them or their positions to look so worried.

'Yes, Nita?' Sanika said. 'Need something?'

'Sushrut is trying you. He's getting a busy signal!'

'I'll call him. We were having an important discussion so I'd put my phone off,' she said, offering an explanation I had not asked for, and then got up and went to her purse and began to look for her phone.

Agashe pulled up a chair and began to type on his iPad. Anant remained where he was.

Then he looked at me and allowed himself a small smile. He picked up his phone from the table and began to check his mail or something. This deliberate lack of attention threw me off a little. Sanika began to talk to Sushrut and I stood there, wondering whether I could stay or leave. Just as I was about to leave, I saw the intercom on the storage unit. No wonder it hadn't been working. It was off the holder.

So silly. I leaned over the table quickly and reached the phone. The receiver was placed on a small pile of A-4-sized papers. I put the receiver back in its place, picked up the papers and turned around to find a paperweight. Agashe was staring at me. It was clear he was debating whether to speak or not to speak. As if guided by his gaze, I looked down at the bunch of papers in my hand. They were the proposal papers for Elena. And the signature on them was not that of Agashe. They were signed: Partho Sengupta, Architect, and under that the Council of Architecture's registration number.

~

'He is worried because of the rain,' Sanika was still in her own zone. 'The news channels are going on and on about the water levels. They're talking about a replay of 26 July. I think I should go now.'

Then she too realized that everyone was silent. Something had gone wrong. Her eyes turned to the papers in my hand and then dropped away.

For a long time, I was in a trance. I heard what Agashe was saying. That Partho himself had taken the lead in this project. They had hoped that Partho was going to open a liaison wing of his own, so the partners would not have to waste time with getting things passed and Partho would also get a chance to be more independent. Things would have worked out fine had all these problems not erupted. He had even looked for an independent office etc, etc… But now things had changed. Partho was not to get an independent office. He was looking at the cancellation of his license by the Council of Architecture and maybe some jail time too.

And Agashe was home free. Which explained why Agashe had been so relaxed. And Partho so tense. But why hadn't he told me all this first? And why had Agashe chosen to put Partho's name on this project over all the others? Had he hoped something would work out? Did Partho accept Agashe's offer as a way of settling in quick? Did I have an indirect role to play? Was it all a coincidence?

Is there such a thing as a coincidence?

According to Agashe, things had spun out of control.

The next day, action was going to be taken against Partho. That's why he'd called me in to tell me. Even though it was late. They were still trying to save him but there was little hope. 'Actually, Partho wanted to tell you himself but he did not have the heart,' Agashe was in full flow. 'He left the office in the afternoon today. I think he wanted to think things through more thoroughly.'

I felt tired. In this terrible moment, Partho had not confided in me. Why?

Agashe's monologue began to fade. I don't know if he went on talking or he stopped. My vision blurred too. Anant seemed to have left the room and Sanika was saying something to Agashe. There was a discussion going on. From the gestures she was making, it seemed like an argument. An argument about what? I tried to say something, to get up. Sanika must have noticed. She began to come towards me. I made an attempt to move but couldn't. My legs had turned to lead.

And then everything went black.

~

The first thing was the sound of the rain—stormy, incessant thunder.

When I opened my eyes, I found I was in the conference room. The room was empty. One halogen lamp was on in a corner but its light did not get very far.

When I looked around, I saw Sanika standing at the window, looking out. The plate glass window was fixed but she had opened the two slit windows at the sides. A fine spray was hitting me. Sanika became aware that I was awake. She stayed where she was but began to speak softly.

'When I was in school, my father always told me a story. It began with a flood just like this. Then Noah filled the ark with a pair of every living animal and set out...'

I didn't know why she was telling me this story but I didn't have the strength to stop her.

'I used to ask Baba, "With such a big ship, he could have saved so many people. Why did he bother with animals?" He would say, "It was the people who brought down the flood when God wanted to wash the world clean. Man was the dirt he wanted to remove".'

Sanika pulled up a chair and sat down.

'I would always ask, "How can all of humanity be evil? There must have been a few good ones." At that, he would only laugh. Today, I know why he laughed. I made a mistake, Nita. I am very sorry,' Sanika said and began to massage her forehead with one hand. I didn't understand. Why was Sanika to blame? And why was she apologizing to me?

'When Agashe and Antya first proposed the firm, I told them we should keep the practice small. There's no shortage of corruption in our profession. And as the work increases, we'll get sucked into it. They agreed and SNA was born. And the practice got bigger and bigger. And we really became one of the corrupt ones. They tried to hide the devious ways that we were using from me. Or I didn't see them because I didn't want to. That was my foolishness or my naiveté. And I don't see myself as either foolish or naïve.' Sanika closed her eyes. Then she opened them and added, 'If anyone could have prevented this, it was me. They might have listened to me but I think I subconsciously ignored it all. Was it my ambition? Or was it because they left me alone to do my part of it? Some other reason? I don't know. I preferred not to interfere. Someone once said: all that is necessary for evil to triumph is for good men to do nothing, right? I did nothing, Nita. I hold myself responsible for what happened today. I am really sorry.'

Sanika got up again and walked to the window, watching the rain. All this began to seem a bit melodramatic. What was the need for this confession now? The first priority was to get Partho out of this mess. We needed to see who could help.

I got up and went to Sanika. But before I could speak she said, 'Partho's gone, Nita. He jumped off the terrace of his apartment block. We just got a call from the police ten minutes ago.'

What was she saying? Partho? Suicide? Why? Fear of the disgrace? Or something else?

'The police want to talk to us. All of us. They won't get here now though. The flood waters are rising.'

I could see that. The cars parked were half submerged. The road was deserted. The sound of the rain drowned all else out.

FLIGHT

TIMES FLIES WHEN YOU ARE HAVING FUN, THEY SAY. LIES. Time flies whether you are having fun or not. I think it's about two years since the day I stopped having fun. As to when I started having fun, that's anybody's guess.

~

Our hostel building was quite far from the college—forty-five minutes by bus, in fact. Our parent organization had three or four colleges in Mumbai. All these hostels were in the same campus. I'm a native Mumbaikar, so I didn't have much to do with the hostelites. But I lived close to the hostel campus, I knew many of them by face. I didn't know all the architecture students but I did know quite a few of them because their college building was in the same campus as our engineering college.

In the first year, I didn't bunk too many lectures. But that day I was very sleepy. I bunked the last mechanics lecture and came down when I bumped into a tall, slim boy. I knew him by face but not by name.

'Gokhale,' he said, offering his hand. 'Rangnath G. FY Architecture.'

I didn't know what he wanted but I shook his hand anyway.

'I saw your portfolio. Very impressive.'

I was thrilled though I worked hard not to show it. At that point in time, my portfolio was my weak point. I had done well in school and Baba had insisted that I try for engineering and I didn't object much. I had got admission in civil engineering but my true loves were my painting and my writing. Not that I was a genius at either but I was rather proud of my achievements in both. I'd enjoyed art from my school days. Before the pressure of doing well increased, I'd even won some prizes and given both the Elementary and Intermediate Art Exams. I was better at sketching than most architecture students, never mind the engineering ham fists. I'd put together my 'best of' in a portfolio, just for the heck of it. Naturally, it became popular in college; most of the students were horrible at drawing. One of my classmates took it to show the hostelites and I hadn't seen it for the last two or three months. Maybe this Gokhale had.

'Thanks,' I said.

'I have a job for you. Will you do it?' Not a tactful animal, this Rangnath. Not then, not now. So his praise had had an agenda, he wanted something. And it had to do with my drawing ability. Apparently, a bottle of Rotring ink had spilled all over a girl's submission, two days before it was due. She was two years his senior. There wasn't enough time to redo it and Rangnath's friend was in floods of tears. Rangnath was drumming up help. When he saw my portfolio, he wanted to add my name to that list of helpers.

I surprised myself by being more flattered than

irritated. That an architecture student wanted my help was a compliment. I agreed to go over that evening.

It was quite late when I got to the hostel building. But everyone was going to burn the midnight oil. At the gate, a young man was on his bike smoking and on the other side, another was sitting on a wooden bench and sketching.

I was about to enter the building when someone called in a long voice, 'Antya-a-a-a.' I looked up in surprise at the first floor, from which a young woman was leaning. She looked more like a schoolgirl than a college student. Puzzled, I looked about and saw that the boy on the bench was looking at her. That must be Antya.

'Can't leave now. Nidhi's submission's fucked,' she shouted so loudly that everyone in a square kilometre must have heard. I didn't bother to listen to Antya's response and entered the building and went to the common room on the second floor.

It was a war room. Everywhere drawing boards, T-squares, rolls of papers, and in the middle, eight to ten young men and women (yes, it was a boys' hostel but Rangnath obviously had his ways) and overseeing it all and giving Nidhi moral support, Rangnath. Seeing me, he got up and said with a laugh, 'You'll have to wait five minutes. Your rendering department in-charge will be here in a couple of minutes.'

And the screaming girl from the balcony walked in. She still looked as small as she had then. She was wearing a T-shirt with the college logo on it and shorts. She grabbed Rangnath by the shoulders and rocked him from side to side and said, 'Ranga, you owe me! I was going to go with Antya to town for Doshi's lecture, but now like a fool, I have to sit here and do your work.'

Ranga gave her a peaceful smile: 'No melodrama, please. You're not missing much. Doshi designs crap anyway.' Then striking a dramatic pose, he looked at me: 'And I've got you a second-in-command. Sushrut, this is Sanika. Sanika, Sushrut.'

That was my first meeting with Sanika, courtesy Ranga. Whenever I think about it, I'm always puzzled. Pure unadulterated coincidence. I can't explain it beyond this. In fact, it's one in a series of coincidences.

If you look at it, almost everything from our personal likes and dislikes to our career choices were different. I was interested in art, writing and reading, but was pushed into engineering. After her twelfth standard, Sanika was going to do a BSc and only on a friend's insistence had she given the architecture admission exam. It was as if things were conspiring to throw us together. Fate. Destiny. That sort of nonsense or at least it used to seem like that. First friendship; then love; next, a live-in relationship. Our bond was so strong, we didn't feel the need to formalize it with marriage. Was this a mistake? Who knows? Back then, it seemed fine. Ironically, that meant we could separate easily too.

Today, two years after we separated, I'm still not used to her absence.

Take today. I had a bum-crack-of-dawn flight to

Delhi so I set the alarm for 3 a.m. In the hasty attempt to turn it off quickly, I dropped two files and my spectacles, all of which were on the side table. Why the haste? I didn't want to disturb Sanika in the middle of the night. It was only after a few seconds of this fumbling that I realized that Sanika doesn't live here anymore. It's been a while since she did. I have to forget those days. Considering this problem, I lay in bed for at least five minutes, staring at the ceiling. Not a good thing to be doing. Not with a presentation at Delhi's Habitat Centre at ten sharp. Regardless of how inconvenient the flight, I couldn't miss the presentation.

I had booked a rental taxi since it's difficult to get taxis in the mornings; the Mumbai kaali-peeli taxis are no longer reliable but then nothing is. When I called the rental service, they said, 'Sorry Sir, we don't have a free taxi in that area,' and from that moment on, the day began to go to hell. I parked the curses I wanted to utter in a far corner in my mind and ran down the stairs. No time to wait for a lift. Now every second counted.

Where I live now is even more isolated than our old flat. It's a little more middle class. Since our old flat was near Evershine Nagar, and close to an affluent area, there were always rickshaws and taxis available. At whatever time. But once Sanika left, it was no longer feasible for me to live there alone. There were many reasons for this, from my being unable to afford it to the space being too large for me. When we were together, money was not an issue for Sanika's firm had been at the top, and she needed a nice place in which to entertain clients from time to time. As a lone freelance worker, I didn't need something so big. But those weren't the real reasons. I had only one reason: my memories. They were all related to Sanika and I just wanted to erase them.

That day it took me about fifteen minutes to get a rickshaw. I had to walk all the way to the main road and even further, half-a-kilometre more to the Shiv Sena shakha where there was a rickshaw stand. One or two rickshawallas refused along the way. One was sleeping; another wasn't, but refused to move. When you talk to Mumbai's auto- or taxi-drivers, you need to have a certain measure of confidence. You don't have to shout, but there must be something in the tone of your voice to suggest that they ought not to have the courage to refuse. I seem to lack this certain something. That shortcoming meant my only option was to continue walking and asking, walking and asking. Just as I was beginning to panic, an auto-driver agreed to go as if he were doing me a favour but he also wanted twenty rupees over the meter. 'Let's just go,' I said and heaved a sigh of relief.

When I got to the airport, it was half an hour to the flight and the counters had closed. Cursing all taxi-drivers in my head, I joined the long line to check identity proof. These systems which are supposed to simplify things have complicated them, but when you look at them from the point of view of the people who create them, you see that the illusion is important.

My identity verified, I grabbed the first airline staffer

I could. I was already too late. The flight was full. After I begged and pleaded, he agreed to put me on another flight with an entirely different airline. I didn't have a choice. With this, I was going to be half an hour late for the presentation but with some frantic phone calls, I would at least try to push it back a bit. At least I hoped so. The problem was that if I tried to call now it would be far too early and if I called when I reached Delhi airport, it would be far too late. As a via media, I decided to send my Delhi contact an SMS and settled down to wait.

I hate waiting at airports, really hate it. No constructive work is possible. Even listening to an audio book is difficult. Either you have to sit and look at the screens or you have to pay attention to the announcements. Flight on time or delayed? Has it been announced? Some shit like that is always going down. Out of habit, I looked around to see if there was anyone I knew and then sat down on a chair right in front of a screen. No sign of my flight for the next hour or so. Just as I was debating whether to power up my iPod or not, I saw him.

Two rows behind me. He could see me but he wasn't looking at me. He was looking at his iPad. Earphones stuck in his ears. Fourteen or fifteen years or thereabouts. Jeans, T-shirt and a blazer for that formal touch. Stylish heavy glasses to which he seemed unaccustomed, for he moved the frame around on his nose as if it were hurting him. I had seen him before. Of that I was sure. But where?

As if becoming aware of my gaze, he looked up but

he didn't see me. He looked around. Then a glance at his wristwatch. He set the iPad aside and stood up and looked around.

He was waiting for someone.

After a minute or two like this, he sat down again. Sat down? Flopped down was more like it. A couple of people sitting in his row bounced on impact and glared at him, but he was paying no attention to anyone. He was in his own world and nothing outside it existed.

I don't know too many in his demographic so it should not have taken me long to place him. I used elimination to narrow the field but his name just wouldn't come back. When this happens, I get a bit restless. But then he did something that jogged my memory. He took off his glasses and began to rub his eyes with his hand. With his glasses off, I knew who he was. Though I hadn't seen him for three or four years, his face hadn't changed much. He was a little taller. That must have come from his father. His father's discomfiture with the world hadn't appeared on his face. Not yet. That would take four or five years more.

I wondered whether I should get up and go over and speak to him. He was part of a world that no longer included me, now that I was no longer with Sanika. Rohan was Anant Redij's son. Antya had been, at one point, Sanika's business partner.

I knew Anant well in those days. He was a straightforward person. But of the three partners, he was the most ordinary. Sanika was good at design. Agashe handled the political and legal stuff. Anant was the jack of all trades. In order to hide this, he often struck a pose to suggest that he was a person of much importance. I met both of them and some of their families too, through Sanika. I'd see Rohan at parties and poojas. He and Sanika were good friends. Sometimes she would talk to me at length about Rohan. He was a very smart kid but going through a very bad phase at that time. Anant was a typical disciplinarian. He could only recognize the kind of intelligence that yielded results on paper: report cards for instance. So he missed Rohan's streetsmarts entirely. I never found out how it had all worked out. Not surprising really. After Sanika left for the US, we'd all lost touch.

One more coincidence, this. I miss a flight and here's Rohan. Antya too? I scanned the crowd for him. Today, memories of Sanika were going to be troublesome.

What bothered me most about our separation was its meaninglessness. We were perfectly happy together. In the last phase, I had been between jobs but that had never affected our relationship. I was entertaining the idea of an alternative career in writing, and Sanika was happy to help. Her firm was doing well. There was a problem with a project, I think, but none of the partners had actually anything to do with it. Later it came out that one of their employees had accepted a bribe or something. He didn't even bear the punishment of his crime because he killed himself. I think that suicide upset Sanika. Or at least that's my guess because I don't remember us ever discussing it openly. We were planning a US trip at the time. The police investigation that followed, triggered by the suicide, cancelled that. From then on, Sanika seemed to lose interest in her job. She didn't say anything, but for the next fortnight or so, she didn't go to work. She just sat at home.

Even when the investigations into SNA were dropped, her mood didn't change. She decided to leave India suddenly, on her own. It's not as if she didn't ask me to come along. But how could I agree, just like that? After all, I too had some thoughts and feelings of my own. She didn't even put it up for discussion. She was going. She had worked something out with some old clients who were going to appoint her as a consultant. I had no say in any of this. I was invited but the decision to go or not was mine. I did think: why not? I could leave it all and go. I might even have got something out of it. Perhaps I might have revived my dormant interest in writing, I could have escaped the boring routine of work but I didn't go.

In this what role had my ego played, the ego I had forsworn? Perhaps it was just anger that she had not talked to me before deciding. But it was also true that I said nothing of this to her. After that, every day till she left, I was aware of my selfishness. But I could not have taken a subordinate role. Just as going was her decision, staying was mine—so what if it destroyed our life together?

Two days before she left, we took our dog, Robie, to

the Lonavla farmhouse of one of her clients. By then, we had almost stopped talking to each other. I felt there were many things left to say; perhaps she did too but neither of us spoke. After we left Robie, Sanika wept for a long time in the car. I had only seen her crying once before. So I had no idea how to console her, specially now with our relationship in this precarious mode. I drove steadily, all the while feeling that her sorrow was not only about Robie. But even then I said nothing. Once we respect the independence of the other person, we have to take it completely for granted. They have the right to make mistakes and we must accept this.

~

Rohan did not notice me until I was quite close. How could he? He had plugged in his earphones again and was lost in his iPad. It was only when I was up close that he looked up and saw me. He pulled out the earphones and stood up immediately. Clearly, he had recognized me.

'Hey Sushrut Uncle, I didn't know you were joining us,' he went putting out his hand. 'Sanika Aunty didn't say a word.'

In the next second, he realized that he'd said too much. But it was too late. I was already looking around. And I didn't have to look far. Sanika was walking up to us—with coffee in both hands.

It was not as if I had never considered the possibility that Sanika and I would meet again; what would happen, what we would say. Not a day has passed without me playing a scenario out in my mind. There's one good thing about these imagined encounters—you get to work the lines for both sides and so it's easy to win every argument; but reality is a little different.

~

It's my fault Sanika and I lost contact. We didn't fight or anything. We had a difference of opinion about her keeping quiet, not about her going.

I could not bear the thought that she was concealing something important from me. In the beginning, she would email me regularly. Lots of SMS-es too. But I would send terse answers back. Sometimes no answers at all. At one point these stopped too.

I hadn't realized it at the time but that fragile contact was a source of support. When the messages stopped, I acknowledged that I'd made a mistake but it was no use. Meanwhile, I began looking for a job. The problems I could ignore with Sanika around all came back, the major one being economic. I could have, I suppose, gone back to live with my parents and job-hunted from there but that wasn't going to work for me. I had to do it my way. Survive on my own, answer my own questions without turning to anyone for help. I did turn to Ranga though.

He was a great help. Whether he felt responsible for having introduced me to Sanika or for some other reason, he went above and beyond the call. First in trying to get me a steady job and then when I decided to strike out on my own. My freelance structural consultancy is alive on the clients Ranga has sent my way. But that's another story.

During this time, I began to feel from time to time that I might eventually get over her, that I would begin to miss her just a little less; out of sight would be out of mind, right? How long could I keep remembering her? At some point I'd break free. As long as she never appeared in front of me again.

Well, this took care of that.

The Sanika who was standing in front of me, turned to stone, seemed no different now from what she looked two years ago. Maybe a little thinner. Hairstyle changed. A little tired. Hopefully the tiredness was not from seeing me.

Perhaps Rohan didn't even know what had happened between us. How could he? He had problems enough of his own. Antya had put him in a boarding school a couple of years ago, and he didn't know much except that Sanika had moved to the US. Rohan's academic record had improved a little in the last two years, and as a reward he was being sent to a summer camp at an affiliated school in LA. Even if Sanika and I were no longer friends, Antya and she were. Sanika was in town to meet her family and she volunteered to take Rohan along. After settling him in LA, she would fly to San Francisco where she was based these days. They were on their way to Delhi for their US flight.

This was quite a coincidence. Just like our first meeting. In that instance it had been ink spilled on Nidhi's sheets, her friendship with Ranga, his knowledge of my drawing skills that had brought us together. This time it was the taxi-drivers' shamelessness, the auto-drivers' laziness that had done it. The coincidence at that time went back a long way. It did now too. I had been delayed because I lived in another home, not very close to anything. I could have traced it back and could have drawn a line that took it right back to our break up which was the main reason I changed home in the first place. So you could argue that we had been predestined to break up so that we could meet again today. Or that we had been destined to meet again and so we had broken up.

Nonsense, right?

It would be idiotic to assume that we found each other again in that airport. Back when we'd been students, it had taken six months for us to get together and now we had about forty minutes. Even though we were all on our way to Delhi, we were on different flights. And things were different. But then we had a long, shared past between us but such shared histories sometimes make things more difficult instead of simplifying them.

What we did manage, however, was a beginning.

Not a spectacular or a brilliant beginning.

Not even an original one. Once you've crossed thirty-five, the chances of doing anything original are greatly reduced.

Now our lives were different. We'd gotten used to living without the other. I had no one in my life; she probably did. I didn't think that was the right time to ask about these things. She didn't broach the topic either. But it was clear that she had no intention of coming back. Forty minutes was not long enough to ask whether her invitation to go along was still on or not. I thought it might not be wise to push too much. I had already made one mistake. I had no intention of making another.

But that day we did manage to take one positive step forward. We did fix our next meeting. Sanika was planning to return with Rohan after two weeks. In a time when much younger kids travel unescorted, Antya's lack of belief in his own kid was unbelievable but it worked in my favour. So we fixed a date on which we would meet next month and she gave me her new number and we caught up with each other. Did she get a little emotional when we said farewell? Knowing Sanika, I doubt it.

Now for a long wait. In my experience, the pain of waiting is an exponential one. When it's for an indefinite period of time, you don't really torture yourself because it stays at the back of the mind. But as it becomes finite, the torture increases.

This pain was going to increase over the next twenty or so days. But it doesn't matter. Time flies, whether you are having fun or not.

When I reached Delhi airport and switched on my phone, it immediately vibrated with an incoming message. From Sanika. The flight to Delhi reached at this time, the next flight was at that time, they were sitting in So-and-So Lounge…just like her old messages.

Felt good.

And as always, I answered 'Okay' and stuck a smiley on it.

I sent the message and left the airport.

AUTHOR'S ACKNOWLEDGEMENTS

ARCHITECTURE, THE PROFESSION I AM TRAINED IN, AND cinema, a field that interests me, are the principal influences on this book. One in terms of the content, the other in terms of form. I am lucky to have discovered both.

I'd like to thank my father Ratnakar Matkari, a renowned figure in Marathi literature, for pointing out the possibilities in a small piece I had written, which got me started on writing fiction.

Pallavi was the first to read the work as it was being written. Her insights are enough to qualify her as a co-conspirator. I'd also like to thank my friends Aparna Modak, Heramb Oak and Vikas Powar. They were the sounding boards for my thoughts during the process.

Suhas Kulkarni and Anand Awdhani, of Unique Features, trusted the story even before it was entirely written. They serialized it in their magazine *Anubhav*. They were later joined by Shyam Deshpande in publishing it in book form for Samakalin Prakashan.

The feedback from Kavita Mahajan, Vijaya Rajadhyaksha, Sanjay Bhaskar Joshi, Arun Khopkar and

Shanta Gokhale was important for me, and continues to be so for my later works.

Jerry Pinto took a lot of trouble finding the right voices for my characters. A big 'thank you' for that! And thanks to Ravi Singh and the team at Speaking Tiger for doing what they do, looking at literature across the language barrier.

TRANSLATOR'S ACKNOWLEDGEMENTS

I WANT TO THANK ALL MY LANGUAGE TEACHERS: FIRST, MY parents of course, and my sister. Then Remizia, through whom I learned what little Konkani that I know.

My English teachers in school, Mrs Adelaide Da Costa, Mrs Mathilda Fernandes, Ms Catherine George and Ms Gilroy D'Costa. The English department at Elphinstone College had some of the finest teachers of English literature I had ever encountered: Dr Meheroo C Jussawalla, Dr Homai Shroff, Dr Soonu Kapadia, Dr Shireen Vakil, Usha Hemmadi and many others.

Then all my Parsi friends who have been trying to get me to speak as *aapri rani* speaks: Jehangir Palkhivala, Mehlli Gobhai and Shirin Sabavala. The French department on which I inflicted myself had some fine teachers too: Dr Mangala Sirdeshpande and Shubha Kamath tried their best to get me past *le subjonctif*. I enjoyed listening to Dr Simone Mascarenhas of the German department, too, when she let me sit in on her classes. My Urdu teacher is no more; but he was patient through the years I struggled with the script.

I came to Marathi much later in life though Mr Johnson D'Cunha and Mrs SY Pradhan of Victoria High School worked valiantly at the adamantine cliff face of my ignorance. And then came Neela Bhagwat who gave me private lessons; and Shanta Gokhale, the best and kindest of all translatorial gurus.

This book is dedicated to all those who try to teach language and literature. Yours is a role we do not value enough. Forgive us, forge on.

ALSO FROM SPEAKING TIGER

BALUTA

Daya Pawar

Translated from the Marathi by Jerry Pinto

'[It has] taken three and a half decades for *Baluta*, the first Dalit autobiography in Marathi, to be made available in English...Jerry Pinto's translation makes the wait for *Baluta* worthwhile. This gut-wrenching, candid personal narrative, marked by linguistic variations, is sensitively interpreted for the contemporary English reader.'—*The Hindu*

'Daya Pawar's *Baluta* has enjoyed iconic status in Marathi literature...The hard-hitting portrayal of the life of an entire section of people from the Mahar caste, who for centuries had been treated as beasts of burden, as far less than human beings, had jolted upper-caste Marathi readers out of their self-complacency in the post-Independence euphoria...Unfortunately, *Baluta* had remained unavailable to English readers for a long time. Jerry Pinto's translation has filled that void.'—*The Indian Express*

'[An] outstanding example of self-writing...Pawar forcefully claims his place within contemporary Marathi literature as a passionate yet self-critical intellectual...Maharashtra has long been home to an indigenous radicalism that challenges caste hierarchies, and despite his reluctance to join a group such as the Dalit Panthers, Pawar ought to be seen as the heir to this radical intellectual tradition that harks back to Phule and Ambedkar.'—*Biblio*

ALSO FROM SPEAKING TIGER

I, THE SALT DOLL: A MEMOIR

Vandana Mishra

Translated from the Marathi by Jerry Pinto

'[A] yesteryear actress travels back in time to the pre-Independence, pre-stainless steel, pre-electricity era in Mumbai...[and] calls upon the reader to devote all senses to the journey.'—*Mid-Day*

'"To us, Mumbai was like a good and familiar friend," says Vandana Mishra née Sushila Lotlikar in her autobiography. This friendship shines through in the book, making it a memoir of an individual, a city and an era, all at once...Like the metaphorical salt doll, Mishra's is a story of acceptance and oneness with time. One is grateful for Pinto's translation. When the author herself acknowledges that the translation is flawless, there is little more to be said.'—*The Hindu*

'Like the best in the genre, this memoir is not merely an account of a life, but of a time, a people and a way of life in which human relationships mattered more than money...[It] is a warm, wise, witty memoir, lit with joy and an unfailing optimism.'—*Mumbai Mirror*

ALSO FROM SPEAKING TIGER

I WANT TO DESTROY MYSELF: A MEMOIR

Malika Amar Shaikh

Translated from the Marathi by Jerry Pinto

'Malika Amar Shaikh's forthright self-portrait—and Jerry Pinto's translation that opens it to non-Marathi readers—is a disturbing yet luminous read.'—*Open*

'[Written] originally in Marathi, [Shaikh's memoir] kicked up a storm. It was not merely the memoir of a woman who had faced abuse at the hands of her husband Namdeo Dhasal, a revolutionary poet and a leading political figure. It also pointed to the contradictions within the Dalit movement in Maharashtra during the 1970s and the Dalit Panthers party that led it. Translated into English by Jerry Pinto as *I Want to Destroy Myself*, the book remains as powerful today, for Shaikh's is the story of a woman torn between the personal and the political, the Left and the Dalit movement, and her love and loathing for Dhasal.'—*The Indian Express*

'[A] searing tale of a promising young life blighted by an abysmal marriage…This translation from Marathi by Jerry Pinto is tender and unobtrusive. The image of "the girl with an unstoppable stream inside" and "a seven-storey laugh" is unforgettable.'—*Outlook*